SEDUCING C.C.

Ariel Tachna

Dreamspinner Press

Published by
Dreamspinner Press
4760 Preston Road
Suite 244-149
Frisco, TX 75034
http://www.dreamspinnerpress.com/

Seducing C.C.
Copyright © 2010 by Ariel Tachna

Cover Design by Mara McKennen

ISBN: 978-1-61581-282-0

Printed in the United States of America
First Edition
April, 2010

eBook edition available
eBook ISBN: 978-1-61581-283-7

To the Amazons

Chapter 1

THE road into Camp Laguna was as narrow and winding as Roger had been warned, the hairpin turns restricting his speed to far less than the posted speed limit, the overhanging trees and boulders making him wonder if he was selling himself into white slavery.

He didn't think so. He'd been told this was the premier girls' camp in the Appalachians, the perfect retreat for a gay college student who wanted a summer free of the distraction of pretty boys. The camp director was male, but he was married and his wife worked at the camp too. Other than him, Roger expected to be the only male on camp property. Except maybe for the dogs. He was looking forward to that. He'd taken the job on a whim when he'd broken up with his cheating ex-boyfriend several months ago. The pain from that had faded, leaving him with the lessons learned and the strong desire to get away from all his friends who kept urging him to get back out and date again. He would eventually, but once bitten, twice shy and all that. He'd wait until he was sure he'd found a guy worthy of his trust instead of jumping into a relationship blind. And in the meantime, he could spend the summer with like-minded people who would hold absolutely no attraction for him on a relationship level. From everything he'd heard, the girls who came to this particular camp had a true love of the outdoors. No electricity, no hot water, platform tents instead of cabins. A lake instead of a pool. None of the pampered sorority types—or future sorority types—who were the bane of his existence until they found out he was gay, and then became his worst nightmare, always afraid he was out to steal their boyfriends.

He rolled his eyes as he checked his directions once more. As if he'd want the type of guy who'd be interested in them anyway.

Finding his turnoff, he drove carefully along a little road so narrow it didn't even have yellow lines down the middle. And then the pavement stopped altogether.

He almost turned around right then, but the sign proclaiming camp property caught his eye and lured him on. He smiled as he drove past the carefully lettered wooden sign:

"Take only memories. Leave only footprints."

It was a slogan he could live by and it bolstered his confidence. If this was truly the lesson the camp taught the girls who came here, he'd fit in fine.

He drove a little farther down the well-maintained gravel road until he came upon the first of the dark clapboard buildings. Seeing other cars, he pulled over and got out, hoping he had found the right place.

Climbing out of the car, he smiled at the rush of cool, fragrant air. It had to be at least fifteen degrees cooler here than when he'd left Charlotte a couple of hours earlier. He sniffed again, trying to place the individual fragrances. Sassafras, rhododendron… and a host of others he didn't recognize.

"You must be Roger."

Roger turned around, a ready smile on his face. "Yes, that's right. I'm the new outdoors specialist."

The woman threw her head back and laughed. "We'll see about that," she chuckled. "Welcome to Camp Laguna."

"What does that mean?" Roger asked defensively.

"It means," the woman replied, "that until you've made it through a summer, you're a newbie, no matter what you know about ropes courses and rappelling, because I'd be willing to bet Seuss knows as much as you or more about them—and about every other facet of the camp."

"Then why am I here?"

"Because neither she nor Spirit, nor Ricki, Rambler, or Yogurt would be willing to take a specialist job when they could be in a unit with the girls," the woman explained. "I'm Ginger, by the way. I'm the administrative assistant slash substitute anything here at the camp. And don't let the Amazons scare you. They're the nicest women you'll ever meet as long as you don't imagine for a moment that you know more about this place than they do."

"Have they been here long?"

"Since they were eight," Ginger replied. "They shared a tent that summer by coincidence and arranged to come back together every summer since. If there's an inch of this old place they don't know like the back of their hands, I've yet to find it."

"You'd think they'd be running the place," Roger mulled aloud.

"Oh, they do," Ginger assured him, "just not in name. Even Scruffy bows to their wisdom if they all agree on something."

"Who's Scruffy?"

Ginger laughed again. "Newbie," she teased. "We all have camp names we go by. You and all the other new people will have one by the end of orientation. Mine, obviously, is for the red hair. It's a great game with the girls, trying to find out our real names. Some people tell them at the end of a session. Other people keep it a secret."

"I've never been good with nicknames," Roger demurred.

"Then we'll come up with one for you," Ginger said. "There's always something. Come on inside. C.C.'s been waiting for you to get here."

"Who's Cici?" Roger asked.

"The EMT—don't call him the nurse—and he also does maintenance around the place," Ginger said. "He's thrilled to have another guy on staff besides Scruffy. Last year, he was the only one and he despaired of us all. Too much estrogen, he said."

"Ginger!" a male voice shouted from inside the screened door to the building. "Stop hogging his attention and bring him inside."

"I told you he was impatient," Ginger said with a grin, leading Roger up the steps to the staff house.

"Hi, I'm C.C.," the guy at the door said immediately. C.C. was everything Roger envied in a man, blond, built without being bulky, confident in himself and his place in the world. "Welcome to Laguna."

"'Cici' like the pizza?" Roger asked, curious despite himself.

"No, like the letters. C.C."

"He still won't tell us what it stands for," another woman, easily the tallest the person in the room, said. "And this is his fourth summer. We've decided it's something horrible that he's afraid to reveal. Not that any of us have any secrets from him."

"Or each other," a third woman laughed. Roger couldn't help but stare at her. Even in cutoff shorts and a baggy T-shirt, she was stunning, her black hair a sharp contrast to very fair skin and blue eyes. Black Irish, his grandmother would've said. "Unless you've come up with one since last summer, Rambler. I'm Spirit. That's Rambler. Ricki and Yogurt are out back making sure the showers are working and Seuss should be here any time now. She had to stop and get beef jerky on the way up the mountain. I swear, she's addicted to the stuff. You've obviously met Ginger and C.C. Scruffy and Brook are down toward the crafts building. I don't think anyone else has arrived yet unless they snuck down to the units without us hearing them."

"I'd think that would be hard with the gravel," Roger said.

Spirit nodded. "It is. We like it that way."

"The girls tend to stay up here during Orientation because it's the only time all summer they get to be together, but I'm already moved into our tent," C.C. interrupted, drawing Roger's attention. "We can head down the hill and get you settled before the festivities start if you'd like."

"That would be good," Roger said. "I don't have much, but that way, I won't be distracted worrying about it."

"Not much like we can carry it from here?" C.C. asked. "Or not much like one trunk?"

"We can probably carry it from here," Roger said. "I've got a backpack and sleeping bag and one other bag of sundries."

"Get him one of those cedar trunks," Rambler suggested. "If all he's got is a canvas pack, the mice will be moved in before the week's out."

"For safety's sake, we have to kill the copperheads and rattlesnakes we find in the unit areas," C.C. explained, "and so we inevitably have a mouse explosion over the course of the summer. A hard suitcase, plastic bins, or a trunk are the only way to keep them out completely. The camp has some cedar trunks that have been donated over time that we lend out to the staff who need them."

"I guess we'd better get one of those then," Roger agreed. "I don't relish having to wear holey clothes."

"I'll tell Scruffy if I see him," Spirit said. "He can bring it down in his truck so you don't have to lug it all the way up to your tent from the crafts building. Those things weigh a ton."

C.C. waved his thanks as he led Roger out the door.

Shouldering his pack, Roger locked his car, handing C.C. the other bag when he offered to carry it.

"So, your fourth summer, is that what they said?" Roger asked as they walked down the hill.

"That's right," C.C. said. "Long enough that the Amazons have stopped double-checking everything I do. Now they only check half of it."

"Are they really that overbearing?" Roger asked, a little worried now.

"Not really," C.C. replied. "They're great girls and amazing counselors, but they know more than the rest of the staff put together about the camp as a whole and our individual areas of expertise in particular because they've grown up here. They could probably hike the trails blindfolded. I've seen them do bed checks in the dark with no flashlights and find every tent without stumbling once—and when you've seen the trails in the units, you'll realize what a feat that is. They can sail every boat here, build a fire with no matches and live off the land without thought. There really is a reason we call them the Amazons."

"Sounds like it," Roger said, more than a little intimidated.

"Don't let it get to you," C.C. insisted. "They won't show you up in front of the girls. They're subtle about it when the campers are around, even if they tear you a new one later."

Roger laughed. "I'm not sure that's any better."

"Our tent's down this way," C.C. said, veering off the gravel road onto a narrow dirt path free of leaves but with roots crisscrossing it frequently, forcing Roger to keep his eyes on the ground.

The tent was exactly as Roger had expected it to be, a wooden platform with a canvas tent supported by a center beam. It looked like it would easily sleep four, but only two cots filled the space.

"Since it's just us, I got rid of the extra beds," C.C. volunteered. "No reason to have them taking up space."

"Definitely not," Roger said, setting his pack on the empty bed and eyeing the contraption over the other bunk curiously. "What's that?"

"Mosquito netting," C.C. explained. "I'm not allergic to them exactly, but I get really huge welts and the buzzing around my ears drives me crazy. A friend of my dad's, an ex-Army Ranger, hooked me up. They apparently use something like this in the tropics. I can see about getting you one if you want."

Roger shook his head. "Don't bother. I've got skin like leather. Mosquitoes avoid me like the plague."

"Lucky you. I do well if I get away with a Benadryl a day to keep the itching down."

"If it's so bad, why do you keep coming back?" Roger inquired.

C.C. smiled beatifically, sending a jolt of awareness through Roger's body. He pushed it aside. What were the chances C.C. was gay?

"Ask me that after you've been through the first session with campers. If you don't know the answer by then, nothing I say will explain it anyway," C.C. said.

"Fair enough."

"Do you want to unpack now or get the nickel tour?"

"Let's take the tour," Roger said. "If I'm going to have to move my gear into a trunk anyway, there's no reason to unpack now."

"Tour, it is," C.C. agreed. "Your Birks are fine for now, but you'll want tennis shoes or hiking boots before you head much off the gravel road. It doesn't take more than a few steps and you're deep in the woods with everything that entails: bugs, briars, snakes, poison ivy."

"I've got boots," Roger said. "Should I change now?"

C.C. paused, considering. "Might not be a bad idea. I heard rumors about a bonfire tonight to welcome everyone back, and that means hiking out to the Point. I also don't know what Scruffy has planned for this afternoon. I haven't seen the Orientation schedule yet."

"That sounds like fun," Roger said, digging in his pack for boots and a pair of socks.

"It is," C.C. agreed. "The Amazons put on quite a moving evening when they put their heads together, although tonight will probably be a lot less formal since the campers aren't here yet. I suppose that's the other thing I should tell you about. This place is steeped in tradition. As long as you appreciate that, you'll be fine, but there's a way to do pretty much everything from meals to flag ceremonies to hikes and campfires. Some of it's procedural, like getting food for cookouts, but a lot of it's more ritual to encourage the girls to invest in the place and the experience."

"I have a feeling I'm going to be making lots of mistakes," Roger muttered as he stood up.

"When in doubt, do what the Amazons do," C.C. said. "If you're doing that, you won't go wrong. Come on; let's go see the camp."

Roger followed C.C. back onto the main road and down the hill. As they rounded a bend, they came upon a wide, open field. "What's that?" Roger asked immediately.

"The flag deck," C.C. said. "See the pole? But it's also the games area and meeting place for all-camp activities."

Roger nodded, looking up at the unimpeded view. "I bet you could see an awful lot of stars out here at night," he murmured. "No light pollution."

"You're a stargazer?" C.C. asked.

Roger nodded, still examining the tree line. "I got my first telescope when I was eight. Astronomy has been my passion ever since."

"Astronomy, huh?" C.C. mused aloud. "Then I think we need to call you Astro. Unless you'd rather we call you Star."

Roger grimaced. "Not Star! I get enough flak as it is without having a girly name too." He turned Astro over in his head a few times, trying it on for size, a smile growing slowly. It fit. "I can live with Astro."

"Astro it is then," C.C. declared. "Now we just have to get the other newbies' names taken care of. I've done my part. That's the dining hall down a ways, if you're ready to walk on."

"Sure," Astro agreed. "The stars won't be out for a few hours yet."

The dining hall was a larger version of the staff house, with the same dark clapboard, screen-covered windows and metal roof, set into the side of a hill. "We store equipment downstairs in the trail house," C.C. told him. "Your ropes and harnesses are all down there when you're ready to check them out. So are the pup tents, extra packs, etcetera, for when the girls go out on overnights. We can poke around in there later but for now, let me introduce you to everyone's favorite people."

C.C. led Astro up the concrete stairs into the back door of the kitchen. "Sugar? Spice? What's for dinner?"

"Nothing for you, you scamp," a graying woman in her fifties scolded, "until you come give me some sugar."

C.C. grinned and gave the woman a big hug and a smacking kiss on the cheek.

"And who's this doll you've brought in with you?" the woman asked.

"Sugar, this is Astro, our new ropes specialist. Astro, this is Sugar, one of the two most important people here. Spice is hiding somewhere."

"She went home to get some cinnamon," Sugar explained. "The truck hasn't brought all our supplies yet and we're making cobbler for desert. Can't make cobbler without cinnamon."

"Definitely not," Astro agreed. "I'm sure I'll meet her at dinner."

"We'll be there," Sugar promised. "If you've got any allergies or anything, or if you've got any special favorites, let us know. We try to keep treats on hand for the staff."

"I love a good cobbler," Astro said immediately. "And I've never met a cake I didn't like."

Sugar grinned. "Then you'll fit in just fine 'round here. Anything you can't eat?"

Astro shook his head. "I'm a regular garbage disposal."

"Spice is gonna love you. Now, y'all finish whatever you were up to. I'm gonna get this chicken in the fryer."

"Fried chicken and cobbler?" Astro asked. "I think I'm in love."

"Everyone is by the end of the summer," Sugar said with a laugh and a flounce that made her look twenty years younger.

"So what else is there to see?" Astro asked as they left the dining hall.

"From here, the road goes down past the units and the craft building and then out to the lake," C.C. explained. "There's a trail out to the ropes course and rappelling areas, and of course all the hiking trails. We don't need to worry about any of those right now. We'll hike them all at some point during orientation. I don't know what order Scruffy—or the Amazons—have decided to do them in, but they usually start with the easier ones and work up. You'll be able to skip some of it since you aren't unit staff. That'll to give you a chance to go out to the ropes course and check out the cliff face and that sort of thing."

"Are you a climber?" Astro asked curiously. "You seem to know a lot about it."

"I've learned," C.C. replied with a smile. "That's what you do around here. When you've got downtime, you pick something that sounds fun or interesting and participate along with the girls. I'd never sailed a boat before I got here, but now I take a boat out on the weekends sometimes because it's so much fun."

Astro smiled. "It does sound like fun. Do we have a lot of downtime?"

"It varies," C.C. said, shrugging. "Some days you won't get away from the course even for lunch. Other days, you may only have one group, or even none. It also depends on the age and interests of the campers. We try to give everyone a variety of experiences, obviously, but the groups of young girls, the eight- and nine-year olds, don't do a lot of the adventure stuff. With them, it's more hiking, some canoeing, crafts, basic conservation stuff. The older girls, though, come for the adventure aspect. They want the caving, the sailing, the rappelling and climbing, the survivalist aspect. You'll be a lot more involved with those groups, obviously. Either way, the evenings are pretty much free because they tend to do things in the units as the evenings wind down. You can always drop in for a visit. The other thing we do is help cover for the unit staff at times. They get a two-hour break every day, but there have to be two adults with the girls at all times, so sometimes we'll cover so they can all get their breaks in."

The sound of a bell tolling drew their attention. "And that's Scruffy, calling everyone to the dining hall," C.C. said. "I guess enough people are here for him to get started."

CHAPTER 2

"YOU up for another walk?" C.C. asked with a laugh when Astro slumped on his cot after he finished unpacking. "We've still got the bonfire tonight."

Astro groaned as he pushed the trunk beneath the metal frame with his heel. "I don't suppose skipping it is an option," he muttered, smothering a yawn.

C.C. laughed. "All the fresh air getting to you?"

Astro rolled his eyes. "I thought I was in good shape, but walking everywhere today has shown me I'm not nearly as fit as I thought I was."

"Sure you are," C.C. said, grinning. "This is an entirely different kind of fitness. Give it a week or two and you'll be all over this place without even breathing fast. And that's experience talking."

"You don't seem exhausted," Astro said, trying not to let his eyes linger overly long on the other man's tight body. He didn't need an unrequited attraction marring the easy rapport he could feel developing. They were roommates for the next two months, not to mention colleagues. The last thing he wanted was for C.C. to find out that Astro was attracted to him and become uncomfortable because of it.

C.C. shrugged. "I learned my lesson the first summer. I've spent the past month working up my endurance so I wouldn't be caught out today. You did a lot better than the other newbies. You might be worn out now, but you kept up on the trails today, unlike some of the others. And I didn't hear Seuss or Yogurt having to give you advice the way they had to help Limey."

Astro had to chuckle. The British girl definitely hadn't found her footing in the woods yet, needing help over every big rock or rough ledge, hesitant about where to put her feet. Astro hoped that would improve or else she'd be a liability to one of the Amazons when she got assigned to a unit. He hadn't studied the summer schedule yet, but Scruffy had said they would start with the easiest of the trails, so surely even the youngest groups of girls would hike what they'd hiked today. "So how far do we have to walk to get to wherever we're having the bonfire?"

"About fifteen, maybe twenty minutes," C.C. replied. "There's a spot that overlooks the lake, where Squaw Creek feeds into it. The rock ledge that makes up the Point is too small to do anything there for the whole camp, but we like to have staff bonfires out there because of the view. Sometimes a single unit will go out there for something special. We've got about half an hour until we need to head out if you want to put your feet up for a bit."

"I'm afraid if I do that, I won't get up again," Astro replied honestly. "Sugar and Spice stuffed me to overflowing, and when I get full, I get sleepy."

"We can head that way now and help the Amazons get the fire going," C.C. suggested. "They'll be out of instructor mode."

"At least if I'm sitting there, I'm less likely to fall asleep," Astro decided after a moment. "I mean, a log bench isn't nearly as conducive to sleeping as a mattress."

"Or to anything else," C.C. quipped with a wink, surprising a laugh out of Astro.

"Had some experience with those log benches?" Astro riposted, dragging himself to his feet.

"Not as much as I'd like," C.C. retorted, "but I live in hope."

Astro snorted. "Picky much?"

C.C. shrugged. "Yeah, I guess I am these days."

"I can't believe there's nobody on the staff who'd catch your eye," Astro said as they started the hike to the Point where the bonfire would take place.

C.C. shrugged. "Yeah, well, what can I say?"

Astro could think of lots of things to say, from asking C.C. what was wrong with the female staff—a couple of them had made even his little gay heart beat faster—to asking C.C. if he was gay. He settled for shrugging and saying, "There's nothing wrong with that."

C.C. laughed. "You may be the only one to think so. I should probably warn you that half the girls will end up with crushes on you. You'll have so many friendship bracelets by the end of the summer that you'll have a tan line around your wrist from them."

Astro shook his head. "The oldest girls are what, fifteen?"

C.C. nodded.

"Jailbait," Astro declared with a laugh. "They'll just have to dream."

"And they do," C.C. assured him, "but they're well enough supervised that they won't get a chance to do any more than that. Most of them understand the limits, honestly. And while they giggle and dream, they're here for the camp stuff, not for us."

They reached the trailhead and turned off into the woods. "This will take us right past the ropes course," C.C. said as they walked. "It's getting a little too dark to see it well, but I can at least point out where it is."

"That would be great," Astro said. "I'll need to get out here later this week, after I've gone through the gear, and check it out as well."

"You should have time for some of that tomorrow," C.C. assured him. "It should be the crafts house in the morning and then CPR for anyone who needs it in the afternoon. Sugar and Spice will hold dinner so they can finish the entire course between meals."

"Thank God I don't need to do that again yet," Astro murmured. "Do you think I need to go to the crafts house?"

"I can't imagine why," C.C. replied. "You won't be there with the girls unless you're covering a unit while someone's taking their break, but even then, it's not like you'd have to do anything but keep the girls under control."

"Good. That'll give me the day to sort out everything for the high ropes course and for rappelling," Astro said.

"Everything should be easy to find," C.C. said. "The girl who was in charge of the ropes last year was very organized."

"That's good," Astro said, "but I still want to check everything for wear, particularly since it hasn't been used since last summer. We don't need accidents that could be avoided."

"Definitely not," C.C. agreed. "Do you think you'll need a hand? I'd be willing to bet the Amazons would help you out in the morning. I don't know what their CPR status is, but I know the one thing they don't enjoy is arts and crafts, so they'd probably be grateful for an excuse to do something else in the morning. And it would be a chance for them to see how competent you are."

"And if we get the gear sorted in the morning, we might be able to make it out to the course in the afternoon," Astro said. "I'd like to go through it once before I take the staff on Wednesday anyway, so I get a feel for the different obstacles."

"There's the start of it," C.C. said, pointing to the heavy cargo net they used to access the high ropes course. "There's a beam, an hourglass, a cat's crawl, a Burma bridge, and the zip line at the end."

Despite the fading light, Astro stepped off the trail and followed the course with his eyes, learning the layout, his mind's eye taking his body through the motions of the obstacles. It wasn't the most challenging course he'd ever seen, but it wasn't an easy one, either. "This looks like a good course," he called to C.C. "Are most of the girls able to complete it?"

"They pretty much have to," C.C. replied. "Once you get up there, it's either go on to the end or go back to the cargo net and climb down. There isn't an out once you're up there."

Astro shook his head. "There's always an out. It may not be an easy or an obvious one, but with a bit of ingenuity, we could get someone down from any point on the course."

"Don't tell the girls that," C.C. told him. "They see it as a full challenge rather than as individual obstacles."

"And so they should," Astro agreed immediately. "I didn't mean it that way. I meant in case of an emergency. If a storm comes up suddenly, which I would think could happen here in the mountains, or if someone were to have a medical issue, I could have them down in a matter of minutes."

"Yeah, the storms don't give us a lot of warning sometimes," C.C. admitted. "Come on; it's getting dark. You can mess around out here tomorrow. Let's get out to the Point before it's too dark to see where we're walking."

"I've got my flashlight," Astro offered automatically.

"I'd rather save it for the walk back," C.C. said. "I don't like turning them on before the bonfire. We can still see to get out there if we don't wait too much longer."

Astro shrugged and left the ropes course with a lingering backward glance, following C.C. along the ridge.

"Yogurt, what did you do to these matches?"

Ricki's shout carried down the trail. Astro shook his head at the sound. Ricki—from her last name, Ricardo, the somewhat stout, Hispanic woman had revealed—sounded quite put out.

"With each other and with people they really trust, the Amazons are terrible pranksters," C.C. revealed in a whisper. "Yogurt's the best. She's absolutely fiendish. But Spirit's the one with the patience. If you play a trick on her, it might be weeks before she gets you back, but when she does, you'll know she's gotten you."

"And everybody's okay with that?" Astro asked.

"They don't play pranks on people unless they're pretty sure the recipient will be okay with it," C.C. assured him. "And they don't play pranks on people they don't like or respect, which seems backward, but that's the Amazons for you."

They passed out of the forest edge onto a wide rocky ledge with a granite point sticking out over a ravine. To the right, Astro got his first glimpse of the lake, spreading out from the narrow cove into the wider body of water. Straight ahead and to his left, the ridges and mountains stretched out in dark green waves as far as the eye could see. He could hear the conversation going on around him, but the view in front of him held his entire attention.

"It's engrossing, isn't it?"

Astro nodded, not looking away.

"I come out here early in the morning sometimes, to watch the sunrise," Spirit went on softly. "It comes up over the mountains, bursting free of the horizon and the mist in all its wondrous glory."

Astro smiled. "There's a reason they call you 'Spirit,' isn't there?"

She laughed. "Yeah, we've all come by our names honestly. Seuss can quote any Dr. Seuss book you want from beginning to end. Yogurt can't start her day without a container of the stuff. Rambler's long legs will take her anywhere, and Ricki's name is short for her last name. Come on; the mountains will still be here tomorrow, and we've got marshmallows to roast and graham crackers and chocolate to eat them with. And Yogurt and I brought our guitars. I'm sure you've already figured out we sing a lot."

"Nothing wrong with that," Astro said. "I've enjoyed the music."

"Good," Spirit declared. "We get a few new staff members every summer who see it as hokey and if they don't get over that attitude, it can really make things tense."

Behind them, Ricki finally got the fire started, and Spirit gestured for Astro to take a seat on one of the logs around the fire circle. Astro hesitated a moment, debating whether sitting next to C.C. would be a sign of any guy sitting next to his tentmate or a gay guy hitting on the only other man around.

"I saved you a seat," C.C. called to him before he could make up his mind. Relieved at having the decision taken out of his hands, Astro joined C.C. on the log bench, shifting around to find a comfortable position.

"Thanks."

"Hey, Birdie," Spirit called with a smile as some of the other staff joined them on the Point. "I haven't heard you mention Judy... Jennie... what was her name?"

"Jody," Birdie said with a laugh. "We're still together. Eighteen months at this point. We're talking about moving toward the northeast when we finish school next year. Somewhere that will let us get married."

Astro's eyebrows jumped. He hadn't expected to find anyone else at the camp who was gay, much less so open about it.

"That's a great idea," Seuss said, drawing Astro's attention. She was shorter than Spirit, but more muscular, looking like she'd pack a serious punch if she chose to, whereas Spirit was long and willowy. He'd watched them today, though, and knew Spirit was far stronger than she appeared. "As much as I'd like to see it happen here, it's not going to happen anytime soon, I'm afraid."

"Obviously, it's a year off and who knows if we'll still be together then, what the job market will look like, all that good stuff," Birdie amended, "but if you don't make plans, dreams don't ever come true."

"Very pragmatic," C.C. said.

Astro was relieved to hear C.C.'s acceptance of Birdie's orientation, but that didn't mean he would be comfortable sharing a tent with a gay man.

"What about you, C.C.?" Birdie asked. "Anyone special in your life at the moment?"

C.C. shook his head. "I'm footloose and fancy free," he joked. "Was that an invitation?"

"You've got the wrong equipment, buddy," Birdie retorted, "and maybe you don't care about monogamy in a relationship, but I do."

Astro's stomach churned as he waited for C.C.'s answer. He didn't want to lose all respect for the other man, even if his interest would never be returned. He'd like it if they could be friends, but he'd learned his lesson from one cheating man. If C.C. was one, Astro would keep his distance.

"I'm learning," C.C. replied softly. "Slowly, maybe, but I'm learning."

"Hallelujah!" Spirit and Seuss proclaimed in unison. "It's about time," Spirit added. "I didn't think you'd ever grow up."

"Don't marry me off yet," C.C. protested. "I'm not ready to settle down. I'm just limiting my attentions to other like-minded individuals, that's all."

"It's still an improvement," Spirit insisted, pulling out her guitar and tuning it up deftly. Yogurt matched her guitar to Spirit's tuning with an ease that proclaimed their long years of playing together.

Before C.C. could say anything else in his defense, or Astro could think of a question to ask that might get him more information about the object of his desire, Spirit asked for requests and settled in to play and sing.

The sky darkened into night, the stars coming out one by one overhead, drawing Astro's intermittent attention as the sparks from the campfire danced heavenward, seemingly urged on by the cheery laughter and quiet singing. The cicadas joined in, adding their own music to the sound of the creek below and the voices around him, lulling Astro into a half-somnolent state, aware of what he was seeing and hearing, but as if from a distance, his thoughts wandering to finding Jarrett in bed with his "study partner." He'd been devastated at the time, having begun to believe that Jarrett might be "the one," but it didn't hurt as much to think about it now.

Oh, it still hurt, but it wasn't the gut-wrenching agony it had been at first when he'd run into friends who'd ask after Jarrett. He snorted sardonically. Hell, for all he knew, the study partner wasn't the first. The friend might be another of Jarrett's side dishes. *Stop torturing yourself,* he ordered sharply, dragging his thoughts back to the present and his new colleagues, maybe new friends, sitting around the bonfire laughing and singing.

"You were awfully far away," C.C. said quietly at his elbow. "Are you all right?"

"What? Oh, I'm fine," Astro mumbled, using the excuse of reaching for a marshmallow to keep from having to meet C.C.'s eyes. He doubted the other man knew him well enough to read the lie in his eyes, but he didn't feel like taking the chance.

He stuck the marshmallow on one of the sticks resting against the log benches and held it over the flames. The white goo turned a light shade of brown as the conversation and the music went on around Astro. He didn't feel excluded—if he'd wanted to join in, they'd have included him immediately—but no one intruded on his silence, either, leaving him to his thoughts as he squished the roasted marshmallow between two graham crackers and a bar of chocolate, making a S'more and eating it.

"You're awfully quiet," Patches, one of the junior counselors, said after awhile. "Have we totally freaked you out?"

Astro's eyebrows rose in surprise. "How long have *you* been here?"

The girl laughed. "Eight years as a camper. This is my first year as a counselor."

A future Amazon, then. It reassured him in an odd way to see a younger generation stepping up to take the place of those who would probably only be there another summer or two at the most. "No, you haven't freaked me out," he said, answering her earlier question. "It's been a long day and I'm tired, but you haven't scared me off. On the contrary."

"Good," Patches said before her attention was claimed by someone calling her name from the other side of the Point. She wandered off, leaving Astro to marvel again at the dynamics of the staff, where a sixteen-year-old girl could speak with nearly as much authority as the camp director because she knew the camp almost as well as he did, and where an older counselor could find herself taking direction from a younger one for the same reason.

He suspected it made the staff stronger and the camp better, but it would definitely take a little getting used to.

CHAPTER 3

"EVERYTHING looks good down here, and that's the bell for lunch," Seuss said as they put away the last of the ropes in the trail house. "After lunch, I imagine you'll want to try out the course."

"That's what I'd planned to do," Astro said.

"Rambler and I both have our CPR certifications already so we'll be your guinea pigs if you'd like to walk someone else through the course," Seuss offered.

"C.C. has already offered too," Astro said, "but I don't mind the practice. I figure you two know the course well enough not to need much coaching, but it'll still give me a chance to watch people go through it and work out all the moves."

"That's what we thought too," Rambler commented. "We'll go as soon as we finish lunch. With just four of us, we can probably each go through twice."

Sugar and Spice made grilled cheese and tomato soup for lunch since it was still relatively cool. Astro ate with C.C. and the Amazons, feeling like their invitation to join them counted as admission to the inner circle. Once the campers arrived, they'd spread out around the room at different tables to make sure the meal and cleanup went well, but for now, they could all sit together.

With the meal finished, Seuss and C.C. went to prepare buckets for the dishes while Spirit and Yogurt led the staff in the post-meal singing that was as much a part of the rhythm of the days as the meal itself. Astro laughed at their antics as they taught the new staff members silly songs to help entertain the girls. Their enthusiasm was contagious, and Astro found himself imitating them as he tried to commit the words to memory.

When Seuss and C.C. flashed the lights, they ended as they always did, with the dishwashing song, and started the cleanup.

Once that was done, Scruffy reminded everyone of the afternoon schedule and then released them to do what needed to get done. Chip and Dale, twin lifeguards who looked like they belonged on the cover of Sports Illustrated, headed down to the lake to check on the boats. Astro, C.C., Seuss, and Rambler left for the ropes course. As far as Astro could tell, everyone else had to stay for CPR. Astro gathered four harnesses and helmets, some webbing and carabiners, and a safety rope, and led the way out to the course.

He was a little surprised when the others deferred to him, having half-expected Seuss and Rambler to take over, given their obvious expertise, but they didn't, letting him walk them through strapping on the harnesses as if they'd never touched one before.

"A lot of the girls haven't done it before," Rambler said, seeing his quizzical look. "It doesn't hurt to let you have a little practice explaining how to do things."

"These are the easy kind anyway," Astro said with a relieved sigh. "We had to learn how to tie them from a piece of webbing as well, in case we ended up at a site that didn't have actual harnesses."

"We used to have those," Seuss laughed. "They hurt like a bitch."

"You think they're bad for you," C.C. interjected. "They're a hundred times worse for a guy. The pre-fab harnesses are bad enough. The webbing ones cut into all our sensitive parts."

Astro laughed as he checked the placement on his own harness. Out of habit, he checked the others' harnesses as well, making sure they were properly placed and tight enough. Seuss and Rambler accepted his diligence without comment, but C.C. wriggled playfully when Astro checked the tightness of his harness where it passed along the crease between his thigh and his groin. "Oh, Astro," C.C. joked, "I didn't know you were interested."

Astro flushed, his hand jerking back automatically, but the other three simply laughed, easing Astro's fears that he'd trespassed. Grinning, he batted his eyelashes at C.C. and cooed, "I've been waiting to get my hands on you since the moment I saw you."

The comment broke the tension, Seuss and Rambler doubling over in laughter as C.C. spluttered when Astro groped his ass under the guise of adjusting the harness in the back. Astro didn't linger long, though. For one thing, he didn't want to take the teasing too far—even if C.C. had started it—and alienate the other man. More than that, he could feel his body starting to react, and sprouting wood in a rappelling harness was a recipe for a miserable afternoon, if not serious damage.

He couldn't stop himself from glancing surreptitiously in the direction of C.C.'s groin, trying to ascertain if the bulge there was interest or simply natural endowment. The harness set off C.C.'s package to perfection without giving Astro any clue as to the answer to his question.

Satisfied they were all wearing their harnesses correctly, Astro snapped a carabiner to his harness along with a length of webbing to use as his safety line and crawled inside the cargo net that served as a ladder up to the beginning of the course. When he'd climbed about two feet up the net, he called, "Someone grab the rope and pull the bottom of the net up so I won't hit the ground if I lose my footing on the way up."

Seuss tugged on the end of the rope in question, raising the open end of the cargo net about three feet off the ground so it would stop any fall before the person inside connected with the ground.

"Thanks!" Astro called as he continued his climb, navigating the swinging net with practiced ease. Coming out onto the small platform at the top of the net, he hooked the webbing to his belt and then to the guide wire above his head, leaning on it with his full weight to make sure it was secure. "Everything looks in good shape," he shouted down to the three people below. "I'm going to cross the beam and keep checking."

"Be careful," Rambler cautioned.

"Always," Astro said as he inched his way forward across the log beam that joined the first platform to the second. It appeared solid, but he stopped several times on his way across, bouncing up and down on it to make sure. He didn't hear any creaks, groans, or cracks from the wood, and he figured he was heavier than the majority of the campers. He wasn't particularly big for a grown man, but the oldest campers were fifteen-year-old girls. He was pretty sure he'd outweigh most of them. If the beam held him, it would hold them.

When he reached the second platform, he switched his carabiner to the next safety line. "The beam looks good," he called down.

The cat's crawl was next: two parallel ropes, approximately shoulder width apart. He knelt down, reaching for the ropes with both hands, inching his way forward until he could squat on his ankles. Moving forward another few inches, he hooked his ankles on the inside of the ropes, his knees on the outside as he worked his way across the challenge. He slid his hands along every inch of the ropes, checking to make sure they weren't frayed. He couldn't find any weak spots. His stomach jumped as he stared down between his hands at the ground a good twenty feet below. He'd have to remind the girls to keep their eyes on the next platform to help them combat the sense of vertigo that often came from having nothing between a person and the ground.

Reaching the other end of the challenge, Astro regained his footing, pausing for a moment to let his nerves settle before switching his carabiner to the next safety wire. He loved the thrill of a high ropes course, the rush of adrenaline that put all his senses on high alert. The only thing he liked better was a round of hard, fast sex, the kind that left his body sated and his mind empty.

The next challenge was, to Astro, the most difficult stage. The Burma loops consisted of two ropes at waist level for his hands and a series of loops for his feet. He would have to step from loop to loop, using the ropes at his sides to keep his balance as the rope around his foot swung in one direction while he reached for the next rope in the opposite direction. He only hoped that if he fell, he ended up between two of the loops rather than straddling one of them. He'd done that once in his training, and it had hurt! Not to mention, it'd been a bitch to get himself untangled and back to standing, and he didn't really want to embarrass himself in front of Seuss, Rambler, and C.C.

"Easy does it, Astro," Seuss called up as Astro braced his hands and reached for the first loop with his foot. "Keep your weight centered over your static foot instead of putting it on the foot going forward."

Astro knew she was right, but it was easier said than done as he stretched his left leg toward the second loop. He could feel his weight shifting and his right leg beginning to move backward. He paused, concentrating on getting his balance again before trying a second time. His foot connected with the second rope and he was able to transfer his weight. Keeping his weight on his left leg as he tried for the third loop proved more problematic.

"A lot of people find they're one-sided on something like the loops. Switch feet on the loop and try it again with your left foot going forward," Rambler suggested.

The suggestion made sense so Astro switched his weight around so he had his stronger leg beneath him and found that Rambler was right. It was easier with that configuration. Not easy. But easier. He still had to concentrate as he worked his way across the eight loops separating him from the next platform. He'd made it as far as the next to the last one when his concentration failed him and his feet went out from under him, his weight pulling him loose from the ropes. The webbing caught him after two feet, keeping him from plummeting to the ground, but his heart pounded in his chest at the sudden drop.

"Easy does it," Seuss called up to him. "Take a minute, catch your breath. There's no rush."

Astro recognized the familiar reassuring patter of someone used to coaxing frightened girls through the process of recovering from a fall. He identified it for what it was at the same time that he felt the encouragement calm his pounding heart and ease his nerves.

When his pulse settled back down to something resembling normal, he started swinging on the webbing until he'd worked up enough momentum to grab the loop closest to his destination. Carefully, he pulled the rope under his knees, waiting now for the swinging to stop so he could regain his feet and continue. From below, Seuss and Rambler called out encouragement, reminding him to go easy and keep his balance. He heard them, but didn't acknowledge them. He devoted all his concentration toward doing the things they were telling him. When he made it back to standing, his spotter-spectators cheered. He grinned down at them, flush with success and excitement. The last loop was easy in comparison, and then he was on the fourth platform with only the hourglass and the zip line between him and success.

The next challenge was composed of two ropes that crossed in the middle to form a sideways hourglass. The difficulty here would be switching his hands and feet from one rope to the other in the middle, where they crossed. His weight would help some, but it required a fair amount of flexibility and balance not to tumble head over heels.

Unfortunately, his center of gravity also conspired against him, but he'd learned to work with that during his training. Resetting his carabiner on the next safety line, Astro started across the hourglass, the first few feet relatively easy because of the distance between the ropes. As that distance narrowed, he worked his way into a squatting position, inching his way carefully sideways until he reached the center of the obstacle. Now came the hard part. Instead of simply sliding his feet sideways, he had to balance on one foot while he transferred the other to the second rope.

Right foot.

Right hand.

Left hand.

Left foot.

He couldn't stop the whoop that escaped him as he made it past the X without falling. Below him, he heard echoing cheers from the other three counselors. Reminding himself not to get cocky, he inched on to the right, coming out of the squat as the ropes separated and he approached the final platform.

Attaining the platform, he transferred his safety line one last time, grabbed the pulley on the zip line and jumped, letting his weight send him flying down the cable toward the other end. He doubted he'd reach the tree where the far end of the cable was secured—the zip line was designed so that the lowest point was somewhere in the middle, although

Astro didn't know exactly where for this one—but he wanted to see how far his momentum would carry him so he could gauge the range for the campers.

"Good show!" Rambler shouted when he came within a few feet of the second tree. "That's as close as I've ever seen anyone come to touching."

Astro laughed. "I take it that's the brass ring around here?"

"One of them," Seuss said. "The other is convincing Rambler to do the trust fall in less than fifteen minutes."

Rambler elbowed Seuss in the stomach. "You try being taller than anyone else at camp—and as heavy or heavier—and see how easy it is for you to trust that a group of ten-year olds will catch you."

"Have you ever actually fallen?" Seuss retorted.

"Well, no," Rambler had to admit.

"See?" she called up to Astro as they threw the safety rope up to him. He hooked it over the cable and attached it to his harness.

"On belay," he called down.

"Belay on," Seuss replied, immediately dropping her teasing tone. Astro unhooked his carabiner from the pulley and let Seuss lower him down to the ground.

"Now, you were saying?" he asked, resuming the conversation.

"Just that Rambler really ought to get over her hang-ups," Seuss replied.

Astro shook his head. "We all have our fears. The ropes courses, high or low, aren't about erasing them, but about facing them. No matter how long it takes, if she finally falls, she's succeeded."

"Ha!" Rambler exclaimed. "Finally someone who's on my side!"

"Who's next?" C.C. interrupted, heading off the incipient bickering.

"You are," Rambler said.

C.C. shook his head. "You know I have to watch a couple of people go before I can," he reminded her. "That hasn't changed over the winter."

"I'll go," Seuss volunteered, "but you're next, C.C., and you don't get to take all day, either. I want to show Astro the rappelling cliff before dinner."

"One thing at a time," Astro insisted. "And C.C., if you decide you'd rather not do the course at all today, that's fine. We'll be out here again on Wednesday with the whole staff."

"Thanks," C.C. said with a smile, "but I'd rather do it once with a smaller audience. It's the first time each year that gets me. Once I've gone through it one time, the rest of the summer is easier."

"You don't have to justify anything to me," Astro assured him. "The only person here with any expectations other than your honesty is you. We want you to try, but if you can't do it, we'll respect you for having the courage to say so."

"I can do it," C.C. insisted, "but after Seuss does. It helps me remember the tricks to the course if I watch a couple of people go through it first."

"Then let's get Seuss up there."

The counselor in question was ready, safety gear already attached as she stood at the base of the cargo net. Astro joined her, checking everything one last time before helping her into the net and pulling it closed as she started to climb.

She navigated the balance beam and cat's crawl with the ease of long familiarity, laughing down at Rambler as she moved through the course. The banter ceased when she reached the Burma loops, but she made it through without any mishaps, impressing Astro with her control of her body and the ropes. The hourglass slowed her down finally, but she kept her feet and reached the final platform in half the time it had taken Astro to traverse the course.

"Well done!" he called when she was on the final platform. "I feel like an amateur next to you."

Seuss shrugged. "When you've done a course as often as I've done this one, you know all the tricks. Besides, I wasn't checking for wear and tear. You could've done the balance beam and the cat's crawl a lot faster than you did if you hadn't been checking them out."

That was probably true, but it didn't diminish Astro's growing respect for the woman in the trees above them.

"Come on down," he said. "It's C.C.'s turn."

C.C. didn't have nearly Seuss's insouciance as he prepared to climb the cargo net. Unlike the other counselor, he waited for Astro to attach the safety webbing and carabiner, once again bringing Astro's hands in uncomfortably close proximity to his groin. Astro forced his hands and eyes not to linger as he fixed the equipment in place. C.C. was nervous enough as it was without Astro adding to it.

"Take your time," he urged. "This isn't a race. You can spend the next four hours up there if that's what it takes."

"I know," C.C. murmured. "Thanks. Just keep talking to me, okay? Keep reminding me and encouraging me."

"That's what we're here for," Astro assured him, lifting the bottom of the cargo net so C.C. could climb inside.

C.C. made it to the top of the net in reasonable time, but the moment he started across the balance beam, Astro could see the nerves reappear. "Looking good," he called up. "Keep your eyes on the far end, not on your feet. You know where they are and where you want them. Looking at them will just make you dizzy."

C.C. had to stop several times as he made his way across the log to catch his balance or regain his nerve, but eventually he made it to the other side. With trembling hands, he released the carabiner and transferred it to the second safety line. Astro watched like a hawk as C.C. spun the screw gate into place, locking the carabiner closed. He was sure C.C. knew the safety procedures as well as Astro himself, but nerves had a strange way of messing with one's concentration.

It took C.C. a long time to even kneel down to begin the cat's crawl.

"He hates this one," Seuss murmured at Astro's elbow. "Come on, C.C! You can do it," she called up. "The worst part of the course for C.C. is the height, and with this one, it's really hard not to look down."

Astro wished he knew C.C. better. If he did, he'd know what to offer as a bribe. As it was, everything he could think of would probably offend the other man if he wasn't gay, and while Astro had wondered a couple of times about C.C, he still didn't know for sure, however much he hoped it might be true.

"Imagine that's your girlfriend lying between the ropes," Rambler called up. "And she's just dying for you to rub all over her."

"What girlfriend?" C.C. retorted, but the words seemed to break his tension as he knelt down and set his hands firmly on the ropes.

"Inch forward now," Astro said. "The hardest part is getting in position. Once you're there, it's only a question of scooting forward until you can get up again."

C.C. followed Astro's directions, his hands moving slowly across the ropes until he was more or less on his hands and knees.

"One leg now, then the other," Astro said, hoping his instructions were helping rather than distracting. C.C. didn't tell him to stop, so Astro figured that was an indication to continue. "Good job. Now hook the other knee."

Astro could see C.C. shaking as he tried to keep his balance and hook his other knee over the rope. He'd almost made it when his balance failed him and he tumbled between the ropes. "It's all right," Astro encouraged immediately. "We all fall from time to time. Just hang there for a minute and catch your breath."

"Easy for you to say," C.C. retorted. "You've got both feet on the ground."

"I fell too," Astro reminded him. "On a different segment of the course, but I still fell."

"So what do I do now?" C.C. asked seriously.

"Can you reach the platform?" Astro asked.

C.C. swung in that direction, but despite having been on the platform when he fell, his momentum had caused the carabiner to slide forward enough on the cable that he couldn't reach it now. "Not happening."

"Okay, then try this," Astro suggested. "Can you lift your legs high enough to catch your ankles over the ropes?"

C.C. did as Astro directed, lifting one leg, then the other, and hooking them over the ropes.

"Good," Astro called up. "Now try pulling yourself up your webbing until you can get the ropes under your armpits."

"That isn't going to put me in the right position to move," C.C. pointed out.

"It'll put you in a different position to move," Astro said. "Trust me."

C.C. did as Astro suggested, awkwardly getting his elbows hooked over the ropes.

"Now comes the hard part," Astro said. "Push yourself up so your hands are on the ropes. And then you can scoot backward across the challenge. It isn't as elegant as the crawl position, but it'll get you where you're going."

C.C. struggled for a moment to do what Astro said, but eventually he got his hands beneath him, allowing him to "walk" backward on the ropes with his hands and knees, more of a crab walk than a cat's crawl, but as Astro had said, it was progress in the right direction.

Astro could hear C.C. muttering under his breath the entire time, but it only took a couple of moments for Astro to realize that not a single curse word slipped out. Astro was impressed. He wasn't sure he'd be able to manage such a tirade and not say anything inappropriate for little ears.

Finally, C.C. reached the third platform. He transferred his safety line, but he waited a couple of minutes before he started the Burma loops. He managed those with credible ease and moved on to the hourglass. He nearly fell a couple of times, but he caught himself each time before he lost it completely. Finally, he arrived at the zip line. He let out a Tarzan cry and jumped, flying down the cable toward the other tree.

Seuss, Rambler, and Astro all applauded before Astro tossed C.C. the safety rope and helped him down.

"Okay?" Astro asked.

"Yeah," C.C. said. "I think I might start in that backwards position from now on for the cat's crawl. It's got to be better than staring at the ground the entire time. Your turn, Rambler."

"Do you want me to go through so you can watch once more?" Rambler asked Astro. "Or would you rather see the rappelling cliff?"

Astro grinned. "Definitely the cliff."

CHAPTER 4

DESPITE the overcast skies and smell of rain in the air, the entire staff packed their backpacks on Thursday morning, divvying up the food and equipment they'd need for their overnight. Sugar and Spice would provide lunch today and then would be off until lunch tomorrow. In their absence, the counselors would spend the night out on one of the trails so they'd all have the experience of the woodcraft involved. With the Amazons as unit leaders for the five units, the real issue was familiarity, not capability, but Astro thought it made sense to have everyone involved, just as everyone had been involved the day before when the whole staff had spent the morning on the ropes course and the afternoon on the rappelling cliff.

Astro had been surprised to find such a perfect cliff hidden in the woods to the north of the Point. At a hundred and twenty feet, it was high enough to present a challenge to all but the most experienced rappellers, but straightforward enough for girls with only a little experience. To Astro's delight, he'd managed to talk the entire staff down the cliff, even the ones who didn't think they could take that step.

It was a big first step, he had to admit. Leaning back, trusting the rope to hold, was a real leap of faith. The descent wasn't nearly as hard as getting into position.

It had been interesting to watch the way the different counselors reacted to the ropes course and to rappelling. He'd expected the same people to have problems on both activities, but that hadn't been the case. Ginger had made it through the ropes course without hesitation, but it had taken her a long time to work up her nerve to go over the edge of the cliff. Limey was the exact opposite. She hadn't hesitated on the cliff, having gone rappelling before, but the ropes course had her in a near panic the entire time she was up there. She'd made it through, though, and that was the important thing.

After lunch, they strapped on their packs and headed down into the valley, where Squaw Creek ran, and then up the other side. The rain started as they climbed the far ridge, a little drizzle barely enough to patter on the leaves above their heads. When they reached the ridge line, closer to the top of the canopy of trees, the rain picked up, the density of leaves lessening and their protection along with it. Several of the counselors—the more experienced ones, Astro realized immediately—pulled ponchos out of their packs to keep the worst of the rain off. Everyone else got wet. Astro spared a moment's thought of relief that his pack was waterproof. At least he'd have dry clothes when the rain finally stopped. The packs that belonged to the camp were of good quality, but they weren't new anymore, and he didn't know if the others would be as fortunate.

He noticed Spirit checking pine and cedar trees as they passed, but he couldn't figure out what she was doing. Glancing behind him, he saw Seuss and Yogurt doing the same thing, which only confused him more. With a shrug, he decided they'd explain later if it was important. Finally they reached the area where they planned to make camp for the night, a flat section of the trail with space enough for the tents to spread out under the trees.

"Don't pitch the tents yet," Ricki said. "Let's wait to see if the rain slows down a bit first. Even if it doesn't, the less time the tents are sitting in the rain, the less likely they are to get water inside." Mother Nature seemed determined to be difficult, though, because as soon as Ricki finished her comment, the heavens opened and torrents of water soaked them all.

"How are we going to make dinner?" Limey asked despairingly. "We'll never get a fire started in this downpour."

"Sure we will," Spirit said with a smile. "It just requires a little forethought. We'll need lots of kindling if everyone will oblige. I know it's wet, but it's still wood and it will burn. Spread out a little and see what you can find."

The staff scattered at her direction. "Astro," she called before he could wander off in search of wood that wasn't soaked through, "I could use an extra hand."

"Sure. What are we doing?"

The counselor pulled out a tarp from her pack. "We're making a modified shelter so we can keep the rain off the fire. Grab an end and spread this out. Do you know how to tie a bowline?"

"Of course."

"Good." She tossed him some light rope. "Attach the rope to the corners and we'll get the tarp up."

Astro did as she directed, the two of them hanging the tarp at a slight angle so the rain would run off one side rather than puddling in the middle and weighing the tarp down. When they got it arranged to Spirit's satisfaction, she, Seuss and Yogurt set to work arranging a fire circle.

"I don't expect sparks to be a problem in this rain," Seuss said with a laugh when she saw Astro's quizzical look, "but good habits are never out of place out in the woods like this. This is forest service land. Part of the agreement that lets us use it is that we'll always practice safe camping skills."

"That makes sense," Astro said, "but I'm still curious to see how you're going to get a fire started in this downpour. The wood's wet, even if the rain isn't hitting it directly anymore."

"We have our ways," Yogurt said, laughing, emptying her pockets of the cedar and pine twigs she'd collected over the course of the hike. "It never hurts to be prepared."

"So that's what you were doing." Astro marveled as he watched Seuss and Spirit do the same. By the time their pockets were emptied, they had a respectable pile of dry tinder.

Rambler came over just then with several relatively small but long logs. "These should do for the frame," she said. "They were at the bottom of a windfall so they aren't quite as wet as a lot of the wood."

"Good," Spirit said, taking them and laying them out to form the letter A. She took a small handful of the tinder and arranged it against the crosshatch of the form, spreading it out so it wasn't too thick. "We'll wait for everyone to get back before we start the fire. I wouldn't want them to think we'd cheated."

"Picking up dry wood as you hike isn't cheating?" Astro teased.

"No," Rambler said, "it's common sense. It's still possible to start a fire even if you don't do it. Depending on how hard it's raining, you can usually find a fallen trunk with loose bark and shred the inside of that. Or you can use a fire starter. We make them with sawdust and paraffin. They burn long enough to dry out the wet tinder, and then it's simply a question of letting the bigger wood dry out near or in the flames so it'll catch too. It may not be easy, but it's always possible."

The others returned, looking more than a little bedraggled. Astro couldn't stop the jolt of attraction when he caught sight of C.C., soaking wet, his T-shirt clinging to his chest, outlining every bulge of muscle. Astro had managed to avoid staring at his tentmate while he changed clothes over the past few days, so this was his first real glimpse of the other man's body. Raindrops clung to his lashes, dripped from his bangs, and flattened his short hair against his scalp. His cargo shorts hung loosely at his hips, the weight of the water tugging them lower like an eager lover. Astro swallowed roughly, trying to look away, but he couldn't force his eyes to cooperate.

"See something you like?" Spirit murmured at his elbow.

Astro's face flushed as he tore his eyes away.

"Don't get your heart set on Dale," Spirit warned. "She doesn't talk about her fiancé because she's very private by nature, but she's madly in love. They're planning on getting married as soon as his tour of duty overseas ends."

"He's military?" Astro asked.

"Air Force," Spirit specified. "They've been together for a couple of years. Everybody told her it wouldn't survive his posting in the Middle East, but it has. He's scheduled to come home in March."

"I'll keep that in mind," Astro said, relieved Spirit had mistaken the object of his interest. He didn't think she'd have a problem with it given her reaction to Birdie at the bonfire, but he still wasn't sure how C.C. would react to a gay tentmate, much less one interested in him.

"I'm hungry," C.C. said, joining Spirit and Astro. "Let's get this fire started."

"We were just waiting for you, darling," Spirit joked. "No fire would be complete without you."

C.C. laughed. "I know." He preened playfully. "I'm the life of the fire, aren't I?"

"Ass," Spirit said with a shake of her head. She pulled out a box of matches safely encased in a plastic bag to keep the rain off. Checking the tinder once more, she struck the match and set it to the wood. It caught instantly. She fed it more tinder, working up to the damp kindling and larger logs the others had piled beneath the makeshift shelter. Before long, she had quite a merry blaze going despite the continuing rain and the breeze that occasionally threw water under their tarp.

With the fire going, Yogurt and Ricki started organizing dinner preparations, and in far less time than Astro would have predicted, dinner was on the fire. The rain tapered off while dinner was cooking, so Seuss suggested they get the tents set up before it got dark, leaving Astro with a new dilemma. There weren't enough tents for each counselor to have their own, which meant doubling up. He'd be sleeping in very close quarters with C.C. tonight. A drenched, terribly sexy C.C.

He had no idea how he was supposed to keep his hands to himself.

C.C. was waiting for him, though, holding the tent and small tarp they'd use to keep the damp away from the floor of the tent. Working together, they set the tent up quickly, Astro's stomach jumping as he looked at the small space they'd be sharing tonight. If they were a couple, it wouldn't matter in the least. They could snuggle up together and let the rain ensure their privacy. It probably wouldn't matter either if they were both straight. They'd share the tent, each on his own side, chatting as they fell asleep. But Astro wasn't straight, and his attraction to C.C. got stronger with each passing day.

"Dinner's ready," Yogurt called, interrupting Astro's musing.

"Let's eat," C.C. said, flashing a grin at Astro as he wiped away the water still dripping from his bangs.

"Sounds good," Astro said, pulling his mess kit from his pack.

Under the tarp, Yogurt was serving a thick, creamy chicken stew. "Chicken Laguna," she told Astro. "Cream of chicken soup, Ramen noodles, chicken, and spices. The stew will warm your insides and the bowl will warm your hands."

When everyone was served, they sang grace and then dug in. Yogurt was right: Astro could feel the chill from the damp and the breeze easing as the hot stew filled his stomach. The metal bowl of his mess kit shed enough heat that he had to switch hands periodically to keep from getting burned. By the time he was done eating, he could feel his spirits lifting. As he looked around the campsite, he could tell the stew was having that effect on the others as well, as conversations became more animated.

After they were done eating and cleaning up, Spirit undid the tarp and built up the fire. "Even if it starts raining again, the fire is going well enough to stay lit unless it's a huge downpour," she explained, "and this way we don't have to worry about melting the tarp. If the weather's bad again in the morning, we'll be glad for it or we'll be eating a cold breakfast."

Yogurt put a pot of water on to boil for coffee, tea or hot chocolate and everyone settled around the fire, both for the warmth and the companionship. Spirit didn't have her guitar, but that didn't stop the younger counselors from asking her for a song anyway. She laughed and obliged, the others joining in, obviously familiar with her repertoire.

"Last summer, they gave her the 'Have Song, Will Sing' award," C.C. murmured at Astro's side. "She hardly even needs an excuse. She certainly doesn't need a reason."

"It's part of her charm," Astro said without thinking how C.C. might interpret his words.

"Crushing on the Amazons already?"

Astro didn't answer, not sure C.C. would believe a demurral. It was probably safer to let the other man think it was true anyway.

Darkness fell, but no one seemed in any hurry to move away from the campfire and into the tents. The laughter and music continued, as seemed to be the norm for the staff, leaving Astro with a sense of well-being he hadn't had in awhile. It made him realize how much of a blow Jarrett had dealt his self-esteem and overall happiness. If anyone had asked him a month ago, Astro would have denied it, but he could feel it now as that stress slipped away in the presence of undemanding company and a true *joie de vivre* that swept him up in it along with the rest of the staff. It simply wasn't possible to be unhappy at this moment in time.

Eventually the fire burned low and the drizzle started to pick up again, driving the counselors inside their tents a few at a time. Spirit asked Astro to help her hang the tarp again. "It'll keep the fire pit and the wood we gathered from getting too wet overnight," she explained as they strung it back up. She made sure the fire was out and said good night, heading toward her tent. Astro went to his as well, kneeling down under the slight overhang of the rain fly, the protective covering that went over the tent and provided a porch of sorts where he could shelter without actually climbing inside, to remove his boots. The door to the tent was open, with only the bug screen closed, giving Astro a glimpse into the shadowy interior. He had to bite his lip to stop a groan from escaping when he realized what he was seeing. C.C. lay on his back, completely naked, hips lifted as he pulled on a pair of clean underwear. His cock was lax, but that only made Astro want to crawl into the tent, take it in his mouth, and suck it to full hardness. Then the tempting flesh disappeared beneath a pair of tighty whiteys, and Astro figured he'd lose it for sure. A lot of his friends, gay and straight, complained about the constriction of briefs, but Astro thought there was nothing sexier than seeing a guy's package outlined by a pair of clinging underwear. Boxers simply couldn't compare.

"Can I come in?" he asked softly, not wanting to surprise C.C. by unzipping the tent.

"It's your tent too," C.C. replied breezily.

It was, but Astro almost wished it weren't. He was pretty much hard from C.C.'s unintentional show and unless the guy was blind, he'd realize it when Astro stripped off his wet clothes. Then again, Astro had just been talking with Spirit, so maybe C.C. would think it was for her. He wouldn't lie and suggest it, but he wouldn't correct that assumption if C.C. made it.

Leaving his wet boots outside, Astro climbed into the tent and dug in his pack for his dry clothes before stripping down. Another time, he'd have gotten rid of all the wet clothes first, but he didn't want to freak C.C. out so he replaced his wet T-shirt with a dry one before pulling off his shorts and underwear and putting on a dry pair.

"You'll be a lot more comfortable if you leave off the shirt," C.C. told him. "Even with the rain, our body heat will keep it pretty warm in here all night."

Astro knew C.C. was probably right, but that didn't make him less ill at ease as he stripped the dry shirt back off again, putting it carefully in his pack so it wouldn't get wet before morning. He slid inside his sleeping bag and switched off the flashlight C.C. had set on the ground between their bedrolls.

"Pleasant dreams," C.C. mumbled into the darkness, his voice already heavy with sleep.

"You too," Astro replied softly, trying to ignore the urge to slip his hand beneath his briefs and stroke himself. The raspy note in C.C.'s voice only added to the arousal Astro was fighting to ignore. He closed his eyes, trying to think of other things, only to have the vision of C.C. arching up dance behind his closed lids. In his fantasy, though, the blond wasn't pulling on clothes; he was pulling them off, his blue eyes sparkling as he sent Astro a come-hither smile. In his fantasy, C.C. was a man he could trust.

It was far too easy to imagine crawling into the tent and covering C.C.'s body with his own, two sets of eager hands pushing aside his wet clothes until he lay across the other man, skin to skin. In his mind's eye, he rocked back on his heels and took C.C.'s quiescent shaft in his mouth, sucking eagerly until it swelled to fill his mouth and nudge the back of his throat.

With a soft groan, Astro rolled onto his side, hand pressing hard against his groin. He couldn't do this. He couldn't lie in the tent next to C.C. and let his imagination run wild when he couldn't even jerk off to get some relief. If it weren't raining, he'd have taken his flashlight and headed back up the trail some, far enough to guarantee him the privacy he'd need to get off. Unfortunately, rain pattered regularly on the top of the tent, and Astro had no desire to put back on his wet clothes and jerk off in the rain. He'd simply have to live with it until they got back to the main camp and he could find some privacy in the showers.

He had almost fallen asleep when C.C. started tossing restlessly next to him. Astro couldn't make out what his tentmate was mumbling, imprecations or exhortations or both, but he did catch one thing clearly. C.C. was talking to or about someone named Lynn.

That was the final nail in the coffin. However much Astro might wish otherwise, C.C. was obviously straight. With a sigh, he pushed his fantasies away and concentrated on falling asleep.

The sound of birds chirping woke Astro the next morning. C.C. was already awake, pulling on his T-shirt.

"So who's Lynn?" Astro asked with a grin. "You were talking in your sleep."

"An ex," C.C. said shortly. "I'd really rather not talk about it."

The flat tone of C.C.'s voice was so at odds with his usual cheerful self that Astro let it go. "Sorry, I didn't mean to upset you. I won't mention it again."

"Thanks," C.C. mumbled, pulling his shorts on and disappearing out of the tent.

Astro shrugged and finished dressing, wondering what new experiences today would bring.

Chapter 5

"I CAN'T believe staff week is over already," Astro remarked as he and C.C. finished their last chore before they were done until noon the next day.

"It always goes incredibly fast," C.C. said. "Do you feel ready?"

Astro shrugged. "Not particularly, but I don't think anything will change that until I actually take the first group of girls through the course. I can't think of a single thing I should do that I haven't already done to get ready."

"Then you're ready," C.C. said. "So what are you going to do with your day off?"

"I haven't the slightest idea," Astro admitted. "What do people usually do?"

"It depends," C.C. replied. "If they live close enough, some people go home. Some people go into Asheville or Waynesville for the night. Some people hang out here. It really depends on what kind of a week we've had, and how much we need to get away for awhile."

"So what are you doing?"

"The Amazons mentioned something about going into Asheville," C.C. said. "There aren't many of us over twenty-one, as I'm sure you've figured out, so we can't do much as a whole staff that involves bars, but Yogurt's birthday is next week. We'll celebrate here at camp, of course, but we thought we'd take her out tonight too. I'm sure they wouldn't mind if you came along."

"Came along where?" Seuss asked, coming into the dining hall.

"To Asheville with us," C.C. replied with a grin. "You'll catch more guys if they think they might have a little competition."

Seuss smirked at him. "You keep telling yourself that, C.C. We'll leave you your illusions. You're welcome to come with us, Astro," she added, turning to smile at him. "We planned to leave around three. That should get us into town around five, five-thirty. We can eat when we first get there and then go to the bar. And we do dress up. We spend enough time looking ratty around here. When we go out, we want to look our best."

"Should I put on a tie?" Astro joked.

"Maybe not a tie," Seuss said, "but if you've got some nice khakis and a button down shirt, that wouldn't be out of place where we're going. Some of the guys wear jackets. We don't see many ties."

"Honestly, I didn't bring anything like that with me, but if we're going into Asheville, maybe you wouldn't mind stopping at my place. It's in Marshall, just outside. I can clean up here, and then run inside and change into something more appropriate than anything I have with me," Astro said. "I'd love to go out with everyone, but I didn't exactly bring anything nice enough with me to camp."

"Oh, are you coming with us, Astro?" Rambler asked as she joined them in the staff house.

"I hope so," Astro said, "but like I was telling Seuss, I didn't bring anything with me that would be appropriate, so we'd have to stop in Marshall."

"That's not very far out of the way," Rambler said, looking at Seuss for confirmation. "I don't see why it would be a problem."

"Spirit said she'd drive us down the mountain if someone else would drive home," C.C. said. "I think she's planning on trying to forget what's-his-name."

"What's-his-name doesn't deserve even *that* name," Rambler spat.

"Whoa," C.C. said. "I think it's time for us to get out of here, Astro, or we'll be part of the man-lynching."

"You think it's okay for a guy to cheat on a sweet girl like Spirit?" Rambler demanded.

"Of course not," C.C. replied, "but you were in the 'lynch anyone with a Y chromosome' stage. It's one thing if you don't agree to be exclusive, but if you've agreed to it, you stick by it. End of story."

"Absolutely," Astro agreed, relieved to hear C.C.'s opinion on the subject, though he'd mostly given up hope of the other guy being gay.

"Sorry," Rambler apologized, though Astro wasn't sure how sincere her apology really was. He'd take it for now, though.

"So you said you wanted to leave around three?" Astro verified instead, steering the conversation away from the fraught subject.

"More or less," Seuss said, seemingly more than willing to assist in that aim.

"Then I'd better get a shower," Astro said. "I stink, and I don't figure you want to wait for me to do more than change clothes when we get to Marshall."

"You don't smell that strong," C.C. said, "and you never know who you might meet in the bar who appreciates a manly smell."

"Not us!" Seuss and Rambler replied in unison.

"Yeah, but he isn't trying to pick you two up," C.C. pointed out.

"Who says I'm trying to pick anyone up?" Astro demanded lightly. "Spirit isn't the only one getting over a cheating ex. I'm going to celebrate Yogurt's birthday and spend some time with some new friends. That's all."

"Spoilsport," C.C. scolded. "Now I'm going to get razzed for trying to get some action."

"Your choice, your problem," Astro said, laughing, though he had to admit privately that he wasn't looking forward to watching C.C. pick up girls. Not when he wished C.C. was interested in him. He'd told himself repeatedly that being interested in a straight guy was asking for trouble, but that didn't seem to stop his attraction. And now he'd get his face rubbed in C.C.'s disinterest. He wouldn't back out since they were going to celebrate Yogurt's birthday, but he wasn't sure he'd make a habit of going out with them if he had to watch C.C. with someone else every time. "I'm going to hit the showers."

"Hurry up," Seuss said. "We need our turn too."

Astro rolled his eyes. "Girls," he huffed teasingly. "Always primping and preening."

Seuss and Rambler glared at him as he danced away from their swatting hands. He grabbed his shower bucket and headed out the back to the outdoor shower enclosure. Honestly, he couldn't think of any girls of his acquaintance who primped less than the Amazons, at least not while they were at camp, but their reaction had been priceless. He'd have to remember to tease them more often.

He washed his hair and soaped up quickly, knowing the girls were waiting to use the shower. The brush of his knuckles across his cock made him hiss. He wondered if he had time to jerk off before they went out, but he decided against it. He didn't know how long they'd wait and he didn't want to get caught if they sent C.C. out to hurry him along. He'd have to find some alone-time after they got back later tonight or tomorrow morning before everyone else was awake.

He'd just finished rinsing off when he heard footsteps on the dry leaves and C.C.'s voice calling to him. "Seuss says you have two minutes before she and Rambler come out here."

"Is that supposed to make me hurry up?" Astro laughed as he started drying off. "What if I want some company?"

"You said not ten minutes ago that you weren't looking for anyone after you got rid of your cheating ex," C.C. reminded him. "Finish as quickly as you can."

"I'm drying off now," Astro said, starting to pull on his clean clothes. "Give me a minute and I'll be done."

"I'll tell them." Astro could hear his footsteps retreating and cursed himself for a fool at being able to recognize C.C.'s footsteps after only a week. He really had it bad, and it wasn't like he even held out any hope of catching C.C.'s attention. Dressed, he sighed and leaned his head against the metal wall of the shower. He wouldn't do anything tonight to draw attention to his preferences since they were going out to celebrate Yogurt's birthday, but maybe next weekend he'd go into town by himself and see if he could get laid.

Pulling himself together, he trudged back toward the staff house, trying to summon the smile he wanted the others to see. He made it through the back door at about the same time Spirit and Yogurt walked through the front door. His eyes widened as he struggled to keep his jaw from dropping. If he didn't know better, he'd swear they weren't the same women he'd worked with all week. Gone were the shorts and T-shirts they habitually wore, sleek tank tops and short skirts in their place, highlighting the lines of their bodies. Their hair, usually pulled back in a ponytail, was loose, Yogurt's sandy blond hair brushing her shoulder's and Spirit's black tresses hitting her waist. If he'd been the least bit interested in girls, he'd have been drooling over them. Even gay as he was, he could look at them objectively and see the attraction. "Damn, girls," he drawled. "Where have you been hiding this week?"

"Under beat-up caps and a layer of grime that never completely goes away," Yogurt said, laughing.

"It's gone now," Astro said with a grin.

"It's just hiding under the makeup," Rambler teased.

"Whatever," Yogurt joked back. "At least I look good when I clean up."

C.C. caught Astro's eye and smirked as the girls continued to give each other a hard time. Astro caught himself smiling back. Gay or straight, their amusement at the bickering was definitely something they shared.

"Ricki's almost ready too," Spirit added. "You two had better hurry up or we'll leave without you."

An hour later, they were all dressed and headed down the mountain toward town, the narrow switchbacks as they steadily dropped altitude enough to make Astro wonder who was driving back that night, or if maybe he needed to offer everyone the opportunity to crash at his place. His roommate had gone home for the summer, so he had a second bed, and his couch folded out. That was still only six places for nine people, but it was better than having an accident on the way back up the mountain.

He gave Spirit directions to his apartment when they neared Marshall so he could change into something a little more in line with what the girls and C.C. were wearing. He didn't look as good as the other man, his lanky, gangly frame looking awkward to him no matter what he wore, but at least he wasn't wearing shorts and a T-shirt anymore.

"We can all crash here tonight if we drink too much," he offered when he climbed back in the van.

"That's a generous offer," Dale said, "but I drew the short straw. I'll have one beer and that'll be it so I'll be fine to drive back. That way we don't have to worry about getting up early in the morning to drive back in time."

They laughed and talked all through dinner, giving Astro a chance to get to know his fellow counselors a little better. He'd already figured out they were smart, capable women in the woods. The conversation over dinner showed him how smart and capable they were in other areas as well. Ricki, he learned, was fluent in three languages and was leaving for Germany two weeks after camp ended to work on adding a fourth to her repertoire. Seuss was one semester away from finishing her degree in physical therapy. Rambler had an internship lined up in the fall as a radiology tech to get some experience before applying to medical school. Spirit would be starting her PhD in history at Rice University in September, and Yogurt had a teaching job lined up at one of the best private schools in Charlotte. Chip and Dale both had a year left in college, like he did, but one of them was at Wake Forest and the other at Davidson on full scholarships.

"I think I'm intimidated," Astro said to C.C. at one point during dinner. "UNC-A doesn't seem nearly as impressive next to that list."

"I'm with you there," C.C. said. "Smart, beautiful, self-sufficient…. What's wrong with the guys in their lives? They wouldn't be single for more than a couple of days on campus there or at the University of Washington."

"We get our share of offers," Yogurt said, "but most of them are more trouble than they're worth at this point. They want what we can offer them, not who we are."

"Isn't that the truth?" Astro muttered, thinking about Jarrett and his lies.

"None of that tonight," Spirit declared. "We're celebrating Yogurt's birthday. Let's get the bill and head to the bar. I'm in the mood to dance."

Their waiter obliged them quickly and then they were on their way to a little club the Amazons knew from the previous summer. It was one Astro had never visited, being far enough from both campus and home that he hadn't made it there before. He could see making the effort to come back, though. It wasn't too smoky, dim but not dingy, and almost the first thing he saw when he walked in the door was a lesbian couple on the dance floor along with the straight couples. And no one seemed to be looking at them like they didn't belong. Asheville was more progressive than a lot of mountain towns, but Astro had learned to be careful anyway.

The Amazons staked out a table, pulling up chairs so they could all sit around it. One of the waiters was there almost before they'd sat down, flirting openly with the girls. Chip flirted back outrageously. The waiter didn't seem to care, and if the speed he brought their drinks was the result, Astro was perfectly happy to let her entertain the guy. He smothered a snicker when the waiter mistook Dale for her, though, and got the cold shoulder. He looked confused until Chip drew his attention again with a wink and a smile to smooth over her sister's disinterest.

"They're quite the pair, aren't they?" Astro whispered to C.C. as the waiter walked off again.

"Quite," C.C. agreed. He grabbed Yogurt's hand and pulled her out onto the dance floor, totally ignoring her protests about having two left feet. Yogurt indulged him for one dance, but as soon as he released his hold on her hand, she escaped and returned to the table. C.C. didn't, staying on the dance floor and moving to the music with an ease Astro envied. His foot tapped in time with the music, but that was about as much rhythm as he could muster. He'd never managed the coordination to be a good dancer, and since the Amazons were still at the table, he didn't feel obliged to embarrass himself.

He tried to keep himself involved in the conversation at the table, but his eyes kept straying back to the dance floor. To C.C.

"See something you like?" Spirit murmured at his elbow.

Astro flushed, hoping the low light would hide the color he could feel rushing to his face. "There are a lot of attractive people out there dancing," he said vaguely.

"So go join them," Spirit said. "No one's going to care if you dance a little. C.C.'s already abandoned us."

"I can't dance."

"Oh, that sounds like a challenge if I ever heard one," Spirit said, laughing. "Come on, girls," she continued, turning to the others. "Astro says he can't dance. I think we should make him the envy of every man in the room."

"No," Astro said, already pulling away from the hands that reached for him. "No, no, and *hell* no."

They didn't listen, and before he could put up any serious resistance, they'd manhandled him onto the floor, surrounding him in a mass of gyrating bodies that brushed against him at the same time that they hid his less graceful movements. He supposed if he had to dance, this was the least painful way possible, particularly when he realized Spirit was right. He intercepted several jealous—and a couple of interested—looks from the other guys in the bar. He wasn't sure how— or even if—he'd given himself away. He hadn't done anything intentionally to hint at his sexuality, but that hadn't stopped him from ogling guys in the past. He'd spent the past week ogling C.C., and *he* was straight.

If he'd been alone, he might have returned a couple of the interested looks, but he'd come with his friends and he intended to celebrate with them and leave with them at the end of the evening. He didn't particularly care if the Amazons figured out that he was gay. They were fine with Birdie so he figured they'd be fine with him. That wasn't the issue. He wasn't interested in a random hookup in a bar, anyway, but he had a strict policy. If he went out with friends for any reason other than looking for a date, he stayed with the friends.

When the girls finally took pity on him and let him return to the table, Astro realized he'd lost track of C.C. while they were dancing. It was just as well, he told himself firmly. If the other guy was cruising, the last thing Astro wanted was to watch.

He'd focused back on the conversation around the table when a flash of light from the strobe reflected off golden hair, catching Astro's attention in time to see C.C. disappearing into the hallway where the restrooms were.

With another guy, if Astro's eyes didn't deceive him.

He told himself it was wishful thinking.

He told himself his eyes were playing tricks on him.

Then he told himself it didn't matter.

Except that it did. Excusing himself, he strode as nonchalantly as he could down the hall after C.C., not sure what he hoped to find—or not find. The hall was deserted, but when Astro pushed on the door into the restroom, it was locked. He glanced around, but there were no exits other than the restroom from the narrow corridor, which meant C.C. was probably inside.

With the other guy.

He pounded on the door a little, telling himself that he wasn't trying to interrupt them; he just needed to pee.

"Fuck off!" he heard C.C.'s voice from behind the locked door. "I'm busy at the moment." The words cut off in a long moan that had Astro's cock jumping in his pants even as he shook himself mentally for being interested in a guy who would act this way. He couldn't even console himself with the thought that C.C. was gay after all, because he didn't want anything to do with a guy with the morals of an alley cat. He'd just gotten rid of one of those.

He almost knocked again, for the petty pleasure of disrupting whatever attention C.C. was getting, but he couldn't quite make himself do it. It wasn't like they were together. Hell, he hadn't known C.C. was even gay until tonight. Or maybe he was bi, since he'd talked about Lynn the other night. Either way, he hadn't known C.C. was interested in guys, so he certainly didn't have any claim on his tentmate's attention. Now if only that made him feel better when the door opened and a man Astro didn't recognize came out, wiping his mouth with the back of his hand as he nodded to Astro in passing.

Astro was tempted to barge in and demand an explanation, except he didn't have any grounds on which to make those demands. Deciding getting drunk was a far better option, he slunk back toward the bar, intending to drink himself silly. He'd ordered a shot of tequila when Spirit appeared at his elbow. "We aren't getting drunk tonight," she told him, though her voice sounded a little slurred to Astro's ear. "We aren't going to drown our sorrows because some guy is too stupid to realize what he's throwing away by cheating on us. We're here to celebrate Yogurt's birthday and our freedom to find someone who deserves our affection instead of the losers who cheated on us."

Astro's eyebrows shot almost to his hairline. He didn't think she even knew he was gay. The others could have told her about the cheating ex, but he'd been very careful to be completely neutral in his comments and not to use Jarrett's name. Then again, maybe that was how she knew.

He didn't correct her assumption about why he was drinking either. She might not care about Jarrett, but he didn't know if she'd be so sanguine if she realized he was interested in C.C. "So how are we going to celebrate?"

"You're going to dance with me," Spirit told him. "I don't care if you can dance or not. I just don't want to be alone on the dance floor."

"So get one of the other girls to go with you," Astro suggested, "or ask C.C. He's a good dancer."

"He's too busy trolling the room," Spirit said with a bitter laugh. "And the other girls are too happy. I want to sway to the music and pretend the arms around me belong to someone who actually cares about me."

"You don't have to pretend," Astro assured her. "I may not be in love with you, but I do care about you. Come on. Let's wish the rest of the world away for the rest of the evening."

CHAPTER 6

"LOOPY and C.C., you'll be at the infirmary table," Scruffy announced as they finished eating lunch. "Birdie and Ginger, you'll be doing Registration. Unit Leaders will be at their shelters to welcome the girls and parents and direct them to their tents. Astro, Chip, Dale, and all the JCs, you'll be escorting people around camp, helping them find their way to their units. Brook and I will be around filling in as needed. Any questions?"

No one had any.

"Good. You have an hour until the gates open. Make sure you get your staff shirts on. And C.C., get some coffee or something. You look like death warmed over," Scruffy barked.

Astro thanked his lucky stars Spirit hadn't let him get drunk like he'd planned last night. C.C. was certainly paying for his excesses this morning.

The hour passed far faster than Astro could account for. He'd gone back to his tent and changed his clothes, brushed his hair, that sort of thing, to make sure he was presentable to the parents. And then he'd walked back down to the dining hall to make sure everything was in order there. Then suddenly the bell was ringing, calling the staff together, and the first set of parents arrived, eager to see where their precious child was going to spend the next week.

He walked with them down to Bob White and handed them over to Seuss and her staff. As he headed back down the road toward the dining hall, he could hear her beginning what was surely a mind-numbingly repetitive spiel about their plans for the week, and her assurance that she would take excellent care of their little angel.

He chuckled to himself as he made it back to the dining hall in time to see C.C. swamped by a flood of eight families all at once. His tentmate looked positively harried as he tried to check their health forms, make sure none of them had lice or athlete's foot, and take their vitals before sending them off to their units. It would've been daunting under any circumstances, Astro was sure, but he could see the lingering tightness around C.C.'s mouth, left over from his binge the night before. Loopy was doing her best to take up the slack, but even with two of them, the line was getting longer rather than shorter.

Astro took another group of girls and their parents—to Redwood this time—leaving them in Spirit's tender care. He passed several more girls on his way back, but they obviously knew where they were going so he simply smiled and waved. They waved back, continuing on their way with laughter and smiles and happy shouts that widened his smile as he wondered what their enthusiasm had done to C.C.'s head.

His continued fascination with C.C. bothered him. He'd just gotten rid of one cheating boyfriend. The last thing he needed was another alley cat who didn't have any qualms about a random hookup at a bar and meaningless sex in the restroom.

His concerns didn't seem to have any effect on his attraction, though. Each glance he got of C.C. over the course of the afternoon quietly thrilled him even as he smirked at the harried look on the EMT's face.

Finally, all the campers were checked in, and all the parents shipped off back home. Camp was officially in session. The dining hall suddenly seemed tiny with almost a hundred and fifty people inside, and Astro's respect for Sugar and Spice skyrocketed as he watched platter after platter of hot food come streaming out of the kitchen and onto the tables for the girls to eat. It was as hot and delicious now as it had been for twenty during staff week.

He shared a table with Ginger, keeping an eye on the six girls who joined them. Watching her and the other experienced staff work the tables, including everyone in the conversation, drawing out the shy girls, encouraging the hesitant ones, reassuring the ones who already missed Mom and Dad, only added to his appreciation of their talents. He had a feeling he'd be acquiring those skills rapidly, in self-defense if nothing else, as some of the older girls turned inquiring gazes his direction.

The fact that he was twenty-one, almost twenty-two, and they were fourteen or fifteen didn't seem to enter into their calculations. He was very aware of the age difference, though, and made sure to give most of his interest to the youngest girls, the ones who looked like they'd never been to camp before. The older ones didn't need anything to boost their confidence.

As dinner ended and singing began, Rambler caught Astro's eye and tipped her head toward the kitchen. He nodded and followed her to the relative privacy of the separate room. "You handled dinner very well," she said. "The older girls are always excited when there's a new male face at camp, but they'll get over it quickly enough, and we keep them too busy for it to be an issue except at meal times anyway. If anyone gets too annoying, let us know and whichever one of us is the unit leader will take care of it."

"I think I can handle it, but I'll let you know if anything comes up that's out of my league," Astro promised.

Rambler's indulgent smile seemed to suggest he had no idea what he was getting himself into, but ultimately, he wouldn't have been interested in any of them even if they weren't way too young for him simply because they were girls, so he didn't figure he had anything to worry about. Jarrett wasn't good for much, but Astro figured his ex's very existence was proof he was gay.

The sound of the girls banging on the tables as they sang the dishwashing song drew the two counselors back into the main room and to their seats so they could help supervise cleanup. The majority of the girls at Astro and Ginger's table knew what they were doing already so it was mostly a matter of watching. When dinner was over, the unit leaders reclaimed their campers from the flag deck, where they went to play games after they finished their assigned jobs. Astro watched from the sidelines, quietly amazed at how all the girls were included in the activities, the older ones helping the younger ones even as they competed with each other. Despite what he'd seen from observing the Amazons and the younger counselors who had grown up at the camp, he hadn't expected quite this level of cohesiveness, especially on the first day.

"Astro!" Ginger called. "Come on; we've got a skit to plan."

A skit?

It seemed he still had things to learn, like the fact that the campfire on opening night wasn't really a campfire but more like a skit night and a chance for everyone to have some fun. The winning skit got to pass off the chore of their choice for the week to the support staff, unless the support staff won. Scruffy and Brook were the judges.

The skits ranged from simplistically funny to sharply witty, and Astro was glad he didn't have to judge them because he wasn't sure how he'd pick between them. Brook and Scruffy had a system, though, he discovered. They started by eliminating any skit they'd seen before unless none of them were original. Then they picked the remaining skit of the youngest group of girls. If none of the skits were original, the support staff skit won by default.

The returning staff all knew the criteria, but it only helped them if they or their campers could come up with something original. As many years as they'd all been around, very little was original anymore.

When the opening night festivities were over and the units were dispersing again, Loopy caught Astro by the arm to stop him from heading back toward the dining hall and his tent. "If you stand around and look pathetic, you might get invited back to one of the units for S'mores," she whispered. "I know at least three of the units are planning on having them tonight. It's a good opportunity to get to know some of the girls and to extend the evening a little longer."

"Thanks," Astro said with a smile, staying next to her and putting on his best puppy dog look. Ricki took pity on him as she walked by, snagging his arm and pulling him along. Right behind her, Seuss gestured for Loopy to go with her girls.

Ricki's campers were the youngest ones this time. "I'll be glad for an extra set of adult eyes and hands to help make sure no one turns around with a burning marshmallow and catches someone else's hair on fire," she confided as they walked toward Pine Grove, the unit closest to the dining hall and the arts and crafts house, usually reserved for the youngest girls at camp due to its proximity to everything. They saved the mile-long walk from Redwood for the older girls with their longer legs whenever possible.

The eight- and nine-year olds, at camp for the first time in most cases, were adorable, hanging on Ricki's every word as she explained the safety protocol for campfires in general and S'mores in particular before sending them out to find green sticks. Astro snagged one from a nearby bush, choosing a higher branch than most of the girls would be able to reach and peeling away the bark with his pocket knife so a fresh green twig awaited its first marshmallow.

Ricki offered him one immediately but he shook his head, helping the girls break off and prepare their own roasting sticks. It hadn't taken more than a day of orientation for him to realize that the girls always came first. Only when all the girls were back around the campfire did Astro accept a marshmallow and begin preparing his first S'more. He had a feeling he'd be sick of them by the end of the summer, but for now they were a special treat and he fully intended to enjoy them.

Darkness had fallen completely by the time Ricki, Birdie, and Captain started herding the girls off to their tents for the night. Astro could see smothered yawns hidden behind little hands as the girls all insisted they could stay up a little longer. The unit staff was kind but firm as they ushered the girls in groups of three or four into their various tents. Astro grinned and then realized he'd forgotten his flashlight. A moment later, Ricki appeared again. "Here's my spare," she told him. "You can return it to me at breakfast. You'll get used to carrying yours any time you leave your tent after dinner."

Astro flushed, though he knew the darkness would hide it. "I'm obviously not the first person you've rescued from their own ineptitude," he said, laughing.

"I've had a little experience, yes," she agreed, shooing him in the direction of the road. "You'd have found your way eventually, but the light will make it easier. Good night, Astro."

"Good night, Ricki."

The smile on his face lasted all the way to the tent he shared with C.C. His tentmate lay stretched out on his bunk, his flashlight directed at a book. "Did you get some S'mores?" C.C. asked when Astro came in.

"Yeah, Ricki invited me to join her girls," Astro replied, reminding himself to be civil. "Now I smell of wood smoke and I'm covered in marshmallow goo."

C.C. glanced at his watch. "It's almost ten now. It'll be lights out for the campers in a few minutes. We'll want to give the girls an hour to make it through the showers and then we can head up and take ours. Now that the campers are here and staff time off is more limited, it's best to wait until they've all had a chance to get their showers before we hog it to take ours."

"I don't really mind waiting until morning," Astro demurred, the idea of sharing the open showers with C.C. more than a little unnerving.

"That's when the other half of the staff takes their shower," C.C. said with a shake of his head. "Unless you want to get up at five or skip breakfast, you'd do better to go with me tonight."

Astro could see the logic of C.C.'s assertion, but damn, he wasn't sure he could trust his body not to give him away if he had to watch the other man bathe. It would be dark, though, so maybe that would hide most of his reactions.

He could hope, anyway.

An hour later, they heard a sharp whistle. "That's Rambler," C.C. explained. "The showers are free."

Astro glanced at his watch. Eleven fifteen already and breakfast at eight in the morning. He was tempted to tell C.C. to go ahead on his own, but that would mean waiting that much longer for his own shower, and he could feel sleep tugging at him. He'd just have to bite the bullet and try not to stare at C.C. too obviously.

They walked up the hill to the staff house, checking to make sure none of the other female staff had arrived in the meantime before taking their gear out to the shower enclosure. C.C. set his flashlight down next to his shower bucket, the beam pointing toward one aluminum wall, the shiny metal reflecting the light to give a faint glow to the entire area.

"It always amazes me how well that works," C.C. said as he started stripping down to shower. Astro gulped and turned away, reminding himself repeatedly not to stare.

The relative position of the two showerheads made it impossible for Astro to keep his back turned completely, which meant that he caught an occasional glimpse of C.C.'s naked body glistening in the dim light as water streamed through his hair, over his broad shoulders, down his compact body and tight ass. With a gulp, Astro tore his eyes away, trying to will down his growing erection. Wetting his hair, he busied himself with washing it, his eyes closed to keep the shampoo from getting in them.

When he'd rinsed the shampoo out and had to open his eyes again to reach for his soap, he caught C.C. watching him with an odd look on his face. He hoped the dim light was enough to hide the flush on his face as he rubbed the bar into a lather and started working the cloth over his skin. He turned his back as he scrubbed at the dirt on his knees from the campfire.

"You know what one of my favorite parts of being gay is?" C.C. asked abruptly.

Astro was so surprised by the question that he spun around in disbelief to meet C.C.'s amused gaze.

"Ogling cute guys in the shower," C.C. continued, when Astro didn't prompt him.

Astro had nodded before he could censor his reaction. The moment he realized what he'd given away, he grabbed his towel, heedless of the soap still coating his body, wrapped it around his waist and fled the enclosure. He stumbled his way back up to the staff house, the light on the back porch providing enough illumination that he didn't run into any trees, even if he couldn't see all the roots and stumps that caught his flip-flops on the way.

Inside, he rinsed off as well as he could in the sink, the cold water raising goose bumps on his skin. He dressed quickly, not ready to face

C.C. stark naked again. C.C. didn't seem to have that concern, sauntering in a few moments later with both shower buckets, both sets of dirty clothes, and both flashlights, his towel hanging so low around his hips that Astro wasn't sure how it stayed up.

"I think you forgot this," C.C. drawled, his eyes running over Astro appreciatively.

"Thanks," Astro replied tersely, setting his shower bucket back on the shelf and grabbing his belongings. "Good night."

"No one here cares that you're gay," C.C. said as Astro started toward the door.

"I didn't think they did," Astro insisted coolly. "I didn't think it was anyone's business, that's all. You didn't exactly volunteer the information either."

C.C. shrugged. "I don't have to. All the returning staff already know. I didn't tell you because I've had roommates freak out on me before."

"Which is exactly why I didn't say anything either," Astro pointed out. He supposed he ought to be glad to hear C.C. confirm he was gay, though his actions in the bar had left little doubt, but his sexuality hardly mattered in light of his philandering ways. Astro absolutely refused to start anything with a guy he already knew couldn't keep his pants zipped. "I don't care if you know. I don't care if you broadcast it to everyone and their sister. It doesn't change anything. I'm here to do a job, not hook up for the summer. Now, I'm going to bed."

C.C. didn't stop him as he left this time. Astro walked quickly down the road, wanting to be in bed already—preferably asleep!—when C.C. returned to the tent. The last thing he wanted was his tentmate's eyes on him as he changed.

Alone in the tent, he slipped off his shoes and shirt, crawling into his bedroll with his shorts still on. He expected to lie awake, the conversation with C.C. and the sight of his tentmate's body in the shower keeping him from slumber, but he was out almost the moment his head hit the pillow. If C.C. returned to the tent, Astro didn't hear him, and he was already gone when Astro awoke the next morning.

CHAPTER 7

OTHER than seeing C.C. at meals, Astro managed to avoid him for all of the next day and the day after that, slipping out of dinner early to grab a shower while everyone else was busy. He was still sitting on the porch of the staff house after his shower on Tuesday when Spirit walked up the front path.

She took the other wicker chair and sat there in silence, not asking him what was going on, not making casual conversation. Simply being with him.

"I was thinking about going sailing this weekend," she said after what seemed like forever to Astro, who had spent those minutes wondering how long he had before the interrogation began. "Scruffy asked me if I'd be willing to take the older girls on a sailing trip next week, and I want to check out the campsites we used last year to make sure they're still viable choices. Do you want to come along?"

The idea was tempting. A night on the lake, away from C.C. and all the stress that entailed. Peaceful hours on the water with only Spirit and the wind for company. Yeah, he could get into that. As long as....

"It would just be a sailing trip, right?" he verified.

"Well, we'd probably have to sleep out on the lake," she said. "I don't think we can get to all the sites and back after the kids leave on Saturday. So we'd have to take tents and food, that sort of thing."

"That's fine," Astro replied immediately. "I meant, well, Rambler sort of mentioned you were single at the moment and I don't want you to think...." He trailed off, quite sure he'd made a total idiot of himself.

"I know you're gay, Astro," Spirit replied gently. "Or at least I'm pretty sure you are. And even if you aren't, I'm not ready to start a new relationship. I was with Gene for two years. I really thought we'd end up getting married. I wanted that. Until I caught him cheating. A few weeks isn't enough time to get over that, even if you were straight and the most wonderful man in the world."

"Yeah, I don't fit either of those criteria, I'm afraid. I just wanted to make sure."

"It's fine," Spirit said, "and I haven't told anyone else, if that's been worrying you. I can't promise they haven't figured it out, too, but it's your business if you want to tell them or not."

"C.C. knows," Astro admitted slowly.

Spirit arched an elegant eyebrow. "How did that happen?"

Astro shrugged. "I don't know, unless I wasn't as subtle about watching him as I thought I was. He made a comment in the shower on Sunday night."

"Is that why you've been avoiding him for the last two days?" Spirit asked.

Astro nodded silently, not sure how much more he wanted to say.

"What did he say? The girls haven't noticed yet, but they will if it keeps up. And we really can't afford to have any kind of tension between staff members," she warned. "So what's really the problem?"

Astro shrugged again. "I don't know how to act around him right now," he said finally. "He's attractive and available and possibly interested, but I'm sort of in the same situation you are. I wasn't together with my ex as long as you were, but I did catch him cheating on me. And then we went to the bar and C.C. hooked up with the first guy who showed any interest in him. I just got rid of a guy who couldn't keep his pants up. I don't need another one."

"Yeah, I see the problem," Spirit said. "You don't want to trust yourself to someone who's already proven himself untrustworthy."

"Exactly," Astro said, relieved someone else could see it. "But it doesn't make him less attractive or less fun, and it's easier to resist if I avoid him."

"Unfortunately, that isn't going to work forever. You share a tent if nothing else," she reminded him. "Unless you're planning on pitching a pup tent on the flag deck for the rest of the summer."

It wasn't a bad idea, Astro mused silently, but he didn't think Scruffy and Brook would agree with him. They wouldn't appreciate the visible sign of dissension among the staff, and Astro didn't really blame them. He sighed. "I don't know what I'm going to do," he said. "It's not like he's done anything wrong. I mean, there's no law against random hookups and I don't even know if he knows I'd be interested. Well, he probably knows now, but he didn't on Saturday."

Spirit nodded. "And even if he knew, he isn't under any obligation to return your interest."

Astro smiled sadly. "Yeah. It's pretty much a fucked-up situation."

"I can't do anything about the nights once the lights go out, but you're welcome to use me as a buffer whenever I'm around. I can pinch you if I catch you staring."

Astro laughed. "That's not a bad idea. I mean, dealing with my feelings is my problem, but I don't want to mess anything up for the girls because I can't act like the sight of him doesn't tie my insides up in knots."

Spirit laughed with him. "He is pretty cute. I remember the sensation he caused his first summer here. Every CIT in camp thought she would be the one to catch his attention. He was only eighteen at the time, to their sixteen, not that far apart in age, so it wasn't a completely unreasonable hope on their part if you don't consider the bit about him being staff and them being campers, even if they were counselors-in-training."

Astro grinned. "I don't have to worry about *that* anyway. The girls won't look at me twice next to him."

"Hey, none of that," Spirit scolded. "No putting yourself down. No, you don't look like C.C., but that doesn't mean you aren't attractive too."

Astro rolled his eyes. "Plain and boring in bed," he said, repeating Jarrett's parting insult.

Spirit snorted. "Let me guess. The cheating ex told you that lie and you believed him. I don't know about the boring in bed part, but I can assure you that you aren't plain. And if he lied about one part, I'd be willing to bet he lied about the other too."

Astro couldn't stop his grin from spreading. "Okay, you win. No more repeating what the idiot ex told me."

Spirit rose to her feet. "I need to get cleaned up and back to the unit before my break is over, but you're welcome to wander down our way if you want. We're going to head out to the Point at dusk and watch the stars come out. I'm sure the girls would love it if you shared your expertise with them."

"I can do that," Astro agreed. "Let me stop by my tent and pick up my flashlight so I can find my way home tonight and I'll head out that way."

"Great," Spirit said, heading into the staff house. "Limey and Pluto are supervising unit chores while I take my break. I'll be back in plenty of time to walk out to the Point."

To Astro's dismay, C.C. was sprawled on his cot when Astro came in to get his flashlight. "Going out?" his tentmate asked.

"Spirit invited me to go out to the Point with her unit," Astro said, feeling defensive, as if he were somehow doing something wrong by accepting her invitation.

"I warned you about crushing on the Amazons," C.C. scolded teasingly.

"And you of all people ought to know how utterly ridiculous that statement is," Astro snapped, grabbing his flashlight and storming out of the tent. He was past the dining hall before he realized he'd probably left C.C. doubled over laughing at his outburst.

He shrugged. Nothing he could do about it now.

Two hours later, Astro was in awe of Spirit's campers. The girls were fascinated by what he could tell them and pushed the boundaries of his knowledge. He'd already decided he would run home on his night off to get some of his books. If all the campers were as interested as this group, he'd need them!

C.C. was already asleep when Astro arrived back at the tent, saving him from any teasing or questions. Grateful for small mercies, Astro slipped into bed and fell asleep almost before his head hit the pillow.

The next morning, Astro skipped breakfast to get things ready for his first group of rappellers. Sugar caught him snagging a cup of coffee and insisted he take a danish with him down to the trail house so he'd have something in his stomach. He nibbled a few bites, but truth be told, he was too nervous to eat much. He gathered all the gear and had it ready to go before the girls had even started on the dishes. When Spirit finally brought them downstairs to pick up the equipment, he'd reached the point of pacing restlessly. She shot him a look that told him exactly what she thought of that foolishness, but she didn't say anything in front of the girls. He appreciated her restraint, though he suspected she'd have a few things to say to him later, when the girls weren't around.

They divvied up the equipment so everyone had something to carry, and started the twenty-minute hike out to the cliff. They had just passed Bob White and were leaving the road when a shout behind them drew their attention. "I've got some free time this morning," C.C. said, sprinting to catch up with them. "I thought maybe you could use another set of hands."

"Sure," Spirit said, her voice less than enthusiastic. Her eyes darted toward Astro, silently asking forgiveness and patience. He could understand her request. She had no reason to send C.C. elsewhere, certainly not one she could reveal in front of her campers, and it never hurt to have an extra set of adult eyes and hands around while they were rappelling. He'd seen enough of Spirit's campers already to know they were a relatively mature group for thirteen- to fifteen-year olds, but they were still young teenagers and rappelling was definitely a "hurry up and wait" activity.

Leaving C.C. at the back of the line of campers, Spirit strode to the front next to Astro, walking with him the rest of the way to the cliff. "I'm sorry," she whispered when they'd put a little space between them and the girls. "I should've known he'd want to come today. Rappelling is one of his favorite activities."

"It's fine," Astro murmured in reply, though it was anything but fine. "It's not like you invited him. Everyone's schedule is on the master plan for the week."

"And you weren't at breakfast so he asked what you were up to," she added. "It didn't take a rocket scientist to figure out where you were once I mentioned rappelling. You aren't going to skip a meal every time you have a group going out to the cliff, are you?"

"No," Astro promised. "Just this time. I was too nervous to eat and this way, everything was ready for the girls."

"Readying the equipment is part of the experience too," Spirit reminded him. "You don't have to do it all for them. They need to learn to do for themselves. I'd be willing to bet Ingrid and Tina will ask you to let them tie the knots in the rappelling line. They learned last summer— they were here for three different sessions—and I'd be surprised if they've forgotten how."

"I suppose if they can do it correctly, there's no harm in letting them try," Astro agreed after a moment. He'd check the knots himself and make sure they were tied correctly before he let anyone descend the rope, and he'd insist on the backup line to be safe, but if they were as competent as Spirit suggested, he wanted to encourage their interest.

As Spirit had suspected, the moment they reached the top of the cliff, two of the older girls came forward, asking if they could help set up the ropes. Astro agreed, watching carefully as they tied the knots with deliberation. He couldn't find any fault. Turning around, he saw C.C. standing there, safety line in hand.

"Here," C.C. said, wrapping a harness around Astro's waist before Astro could protest. He drew the line at letting C.C. slip the leg straps between his legs and around his thighs.

"I can strap my own harness," Astro snapped. "If you insist on helping, see how the girls are doing."

"What fun is that?" C.C. murmured as he stepped back. Astro scowled, but left it alone since C.C. backed off. Spirit sent him another apologetic look, but there wasn't really anything she could do. Astro figured he could shout sexual harassment but that wouldn't solve anything, either, except to turn the summer into a war zone and he didn't want that. He wished again that C.C. was the kind of man he could truly have a relationship with rather than one who slept around. Things would be so much easier that way.

C.C. kept up his silent campaign, though, intruding in Astro's space constantly, always under the guise of helping him with something while using that as an excuse to touch him. Each individual touch was barely noticeable but after three hours of that, every inch of Astro's skin had grown sensitive and his whole body ached with need. He tried his best to ignore it, but he doubted he was successful. The girls didn't seem to notice, but Astro didn't delude himself into thinking C.C. was as naively unaware, not when Astro could feel the harness cutting into his legs more tightly as the morning wore on. The constriction kept him from getting fully hard, but he was definitely moving in that direction.

Finally the last girl finished her descent, and Astro offered the remaining staff the chance to rappel. Limey wasn't interested so she started back toward the unit with the campers while Pluto took her turn, leaving Astro alone with C.C.

"What the hell are you doing?" Astro demanded when Pluto had descended out of earshot.

"Trying to get your attention," C.C. replied, as if that were the most obvious thing in the world.

"Did it ever occur to you that I might need to concentrate on my job?" Astro demanded.

C.C. shrugged. "You're good. You were fine."

"That isn't your choice to make," Astro protested. "The girls deserved my full attention."

"Fine," C.C. said with a roll of his eyes. "Send me down the cliff."

Astro grabbed the D-ring and attached it to C.C.'s carabiner. He called down to Spirit to let her know C.C. was ready.

"Belay on," she called back from the bottom of the cliff.

Astro refused to let his hands linger as he fastened the back-up line to C.C.'s harness, the rope tied through the D-ring attached to his own harness, which was attached to the safety line around a large tree. He doubted C.C. needed the safety line given the ease with which he backed over the cliff, but Astro didn't want to take any chances on the main rope failing. He'd checked it when he first got to camp, again before he'd taken the staff rappelling, and yet again this morning, but that didn't change the basic tenets of safety.

The rope fed through his fingers and the D-ring as C.C. worked his way steadily down the cliff. When C.C. reached the base of the cliff, Spirit called back up to him, asking him if he wanted a chance as well. He was tempted, but in the end, he declined. Lunch would be ready sooner rather than later, and now that his nerves from the morning had settled, he was hungry.

"No thanks," he called back down to her. "I'll start packing up the gear while you hike back around. I'll meet you on the trail."

"Okay, see you in a few minutes," Spirit said.

Alone finally, Astro undid the safety line and removed his harness, sinking to the ground once it was off. He could feel the blood flowing more freely again, his legs tingling a little now that the constriction of the harness was removed. He scrubbed his palms over his face, smearing sweat and dirt as he tried to settle his nerves. He was acting like a teenager with his first crush—despite being well past that stage—and he didn't like it. At all.

He also couldn't seem to help it. His heart had started racing the moment he heard C.C.'s voice on the trail that morning and it had picked up again every time C.C. touched him or spoke to him. The girls hadn't noticed because they were too excited about rappelling to pay attention to him beyond his instructions for safety. Limey and Pluto didn't know him well enough to read his reactions. He suspected Spirit would've noticed if she hadn't been belaying from the bottom of the cliff. Most important, though, was whether C.C. had noticed. Astro couldn't decide what he hoped the answer was to that question.

He'd told himself repeatedly that he didn't want another playboy who would think nothing of running around behind his back, and he meant it, but his memory dredged up C.C.'s firm agreement with Rambler and Seuss when they'd discussed Spirit's cheating ex. He hoped that meant C.C.'s tomcatting was limited to times when he was between boyfriends, and last Saturday, C.C. hadn't even known for sure Astro was gay, much less that he might be interested. He had no reason not to have found congenial company at the bar. Astro simply wished he didn't have that image in his head: it was too close to the memory of having walked in on Jarrett with another guy.

With a sigh, Astro rocked to his feet and started coiling the two ropes. Limey and the girls had taken all the extra harnesses, D-rings and carabiners back to the equipment shed already. All that remained was the equipment he'd been using. When he had it all ready to go, he started back toward the main trail, reminding himself that he was there to work, not to get involved in a new relationship before he was barely over the old one.

Unfortunately, his libido had other ideas, his body reacting the moment he heard C.C.'s voice coming down the trail as he teased Spirit about something. He couldn't hear her reply, but he caught the acerbic tone of her voice and decided he was glad she'd directed that at C.C. rather than at him.

"Come on, Astro," C.C. said as soon as he was in sight. "Tell Spirit I'm right."

"I don't know," Astro said, hesitating. "I'm not sure I want to get on her bad side. I've heard stories about Spirit and her revenge."

"And every one of them is true," Spirit replied ominously.

"Spirit's right," Astro said with mock seriousness. "Whatever it was, I'm quite sure she's right."

Spirit's peal of laughter drowned out the buzzing of the insects in Astro's ears, bringing a smile to his face as he fell in step beside them. C.C. spluttered, only adding to Spirit's mirth.

Astro grinned all the way back to the dining hall, feeling much less alone suddenly. Maybe he could do this after all. He just had to keep things in perspective.

CHAPTER 8

ASTRO was surprised at how quickly the week had passed. It was already Friday night and the girls would be going home after breakfast in the morning. At dinner the girls had been all abuzz about the campfire and all it would entail. After listening to the older girls talk, Astro was curious to see how the closing campfire would go. They seemed to expect quite a show.

"Astro!"

Astro looked up to see another little girl, one he'd sat with at lunch a few times, come running up to him.

"I made this for you," she said, handing him a woven friendship bracelet. "I'll never forget you."

Much to Astro's embarrassment, it took him a minute to remember her name. "Thank you, Anita. That was very kind of you." He took the bracelet and tied it around his wrist, adding it to the growing collection on his arm. He didn't have anywhere near the number the Amazons did, but he thought he'd done pretty well for his first week at camp. He'd miss these girls, he realized. He knew another group would come on Sunday and he was sure they'd be just as great, but this group was special—his first group of campers. He could hear C.C. now, making some obnoxious comment about him losing his camp cherry. Honestly, he thought he would remember these girls with the same kind of affection he still had for his first lover. He and Kyle hadn't been together in three years, but thoughts of him still brought a smile to Astro's face. These girls would do the same.

He fingered one of the bracelets, this one made of plastic string in his favorite colors. Patricia, one of Seuss's campers, had given it to him at lunch, telling him as she did that this was the third summer she'd been allowed to go rappelling, but the first time she'd managed to back over the cliff. Always before, she had panicked and chickened out. She gave him a big hug and promised to write to him often. Astro hadn't known what to say to that, but he'd dutifully written his address in her book beneath all the Amazons' names. He figured that if they felt comfortable giving that information then he could too.

"Ready for the campfire?" Ginger asked as the unit staff collected their campers from the flag deck.

"What time does it start?" he inquired. "If Scruffy said, I didn't hear him."

"He probably didn't say," Ginger commented. "It's always at eight-thirty so he probably figured C.C. would get you there."

"Yeah," Astro agreed, not mentioning that he and C.C. were hardly talking at the moment. It was bad enough that Spirit knew. He didn't want to polarize the staff over something as stupid as his unresolved feelings for C.C. It wasn't anyone's problem but his own.

"Don't forget some tissues," Ginger added as she walked away. "Even if you don't need them, you'll want them for the girls who are crying on your shoulder after it's over."

Three hours later, he was glad of Ginger's advice. He'd lost track of how many girls had cried on his shoulder at the thought of leaving camp and not seeing him again until next summer. He hugged them all, but he was careful not to make any promises. He didn't know what the rest of this summer would bring, much less where he'd be this time next year.

The last girls were finally persuaded to head back to their tents. "It's always hard to see them go," Loopy said quietly. "Their lives are centered around this place for the moment and they feel like the world's about to end. They'll get home and meet back up with their school friends and before long, everything will be back in proper perspective. We'll be a happy memory, nothing more."

The words, surely intended to be comforting, left Astro feeling chilled. He hadn't thought about the summer ending, not really, but they'd only be at the camp for nine and a half weeks, and two weeks of that was already gone. A summer seemed like forever when it started, but he knew from experience how fast that time really went. Depending on how things went next year at school, he might never see the people he met at camp again. He might never see C.C. again.

Of course that assumed he wanted to see C.C. again after the summer ended, but the thought that life might not give him a choice bothered him. He drifted toward the staff house, not sure who would be up there at this time of night on closing night, but he knew he didn't want to be alone.

C.C. was already up there, sprawled in the hammock stretched between two of the support posts on the porch. Brook was there as well, surprising Astro. He didn't think he'd ever seen the camp's program director up at the staff house. He didn't know where she and Scruffy took their showers—he thought the staff house had the only hot shower on the property and he couldn't imagine voluntarily taking cold showers all the time—but he hadn't seen either of them at the staff house since the first day. "Did you enjoy the campfire?" Brook asked as Astro took a seat in one of the wooden rockers.

"I did," Astro said. "I was surprised by the thought of how much I'll miss the girls."

Brook nodded. "We always make comments about new ones coming on Sunday, but each group is special and good-byes are always hard. Some of them will be back again later in the summer; some won't come back until next summer; some won't be back at all. It's one of the challenges of working here."

"And some will come back every summer for as long as they can," Ricki said, stepping onto the porch out of the darkness. "For some of the girls, like for some of the staff, this place grabs hold of them—of us— and doesn't let go. Ever. Last summer, we had a visit from a counselor who was here my second year as a camper. She'd had to stop working at camp because of some health problems, but she never stopped loving it out here and she wanted to come see how much it had changed."

"Had it?" Astro asked curiously.

"A little," Ricki said. "The staff showers had been rebuilt. The dining hall has a new roof. The shelter in Pine Grove was moved after a tree fell on it in a windstorm. We didn't have the ropes course yet when she worked here. But she said the spirit of the place was exactly as she remembered. A place of peace and refuge for anyone who needs it."

As silence descended for a moment, broken only by the night sounds of the pine branches rustling in the wind and the cicadas whirring with all their might, Astro pondered Ricki's words. He'd come here hoping for exactly what she described. A place to lick his wounds and let his heart finish recovering. He hadn't counted on the distraction of another male counselor, much less another gay male counselor, but he hadn't seen all that much of C.C. during the week, except at night, and even then, he'd managed to keep that from being too much of a distraction. As he reflected on the week, he realized he did feel stronger than he had when he arrived. Being outside, being with the girls, flowing through the ritual of the days, full of laughter and cheer and excitement and triumph, was doing the work he'd hoped it would. He *was* better than he'd been when he arrived.

Resting his head against the back of the rocking chair, Astro closed his eyes, a smile playing across his lips as he let the rest of the summer stretch out before him, an oasis, as Ricki had said, a long, healing balm to his battered heart.

A few at a time, the rest of the staff drifted in and out, taking showers, grabbing a snack from their separate stashes, or simply enjoying a few minutes with the other counselors, but the comings and goings didn't disturb Astro's peace. Instead, they provided a soothing backdrop to the sense of calm and safety that encompassed him. Occasionally his eyes would drift to C.C., all but asleep in the hammock, but at the moment, even that sight didn't disrupt his equilibrium. For the moment, C.C. was another part of that equation, a part of this time and place as much as anyone else, and Astro found that thought oddly comforting. After all, without C.C. there to ruffle his feathers, he might never have confided in Spirit the way he'd done the other night, might never have made the connection that he could already sense building into a real friendship. He was looking forward to the hours on the lake with her tomorrow and Sunday morning, adding to that friendship.

ALL Astro's doubts and worries came rushing back the next morning as girls who had tearfully lamented the session's ending the night before ran eagerly to their parents, rushing into their cars with cell phones and iPods in hand again, already on their way back to their everyday lives. A lot of them asked for Astro's address—along with the addresses of most of the rest of the staff—before they left, but he could feel the magic of the previous night slipping away with each good-bye, the fragility of the connections they'd made no match for the lure of the outside world.

"How many of them will actually write?" he asked Rambler after he'd written his address for what seemed like the hundredth time.

"You'll get a few letters here during the summer," Rambler said, "but once they get back to school in the fall, I'd be surprised if you get more than one or two. They all leave with the best of intentions, but letter writing is a lost art these days, and they get busy and have more important things to do. And honestly, that's as it should be. Camp is a wonderful experience for them, but it's a week out of their year."

And only nine weeks out of his, Astro reminded himself silently, his heart sinking at the thought. He needed to remember that, to keep things in perspective.

An hour later, after all the girls had left, C.C. joined Astro on the bench of the picnic table where he'd been helping with Checkout. "I was thinking about heading back into town for the evening," he said. "Care to join me? I know a bar where we could get some action, no questions asked and no one to look at us sideways."

"I'm going sailing with Spirit," Astro said, his voice rough with derision. He pushed away from the table, ready to stalk off, but he couldn't make himself leave quite so coldly. He didn't want any part of going to a bar and watching C.C. pick up other men, but neither could he simply walk away. "Be safe," he added, shoulders slumping at the thought of C.C. doing anything that might require precautions with anyone but him. He might not want a relationship with a man who slept around, but he couldn't deny the attraction to this one in particular.

Astro found Spirit in the dining hall, making sandwiches. On the table next to her was a pile of other food: instant oatmeal packages, canned soup, a package of lemonade mix, a bag of trail mix, and a package of cookies. "What, no marshmallows?" he teased.

"You just wait," she threatened playfully. "You have no idea how many S'mores you'll eat before the summer's over. I prefer to save mine for the nights when I have no choice. Otherwise, I get to the point that I can't even choke them down."

Astro couldn't imagine, but he took her at her word. She certainly had the experience to know. "So when are we heading out?"

"I need to get my blankets together," she said. "Even with a tent, it's too cool not to have something at night. Could you grab two tents and a couple of the waterproof bags from the trail house? I think once we get those loaded with our food and gear, we'll be ready to go."

"Sure," Astro said. He gathered the gear, tossed his own bedroll and a change of clothes inside one of the bags and went back to the dining hall to pack up the food. Spirit wasn't there, so he figured she'd gone back to her tent to get her own blankets. Fortunately, the walk to Pine Grove wasn't all that long. He went ahead and divided the food between the two dry bags, leaving space for Spirit's gear in the other bag.

"Oh, good," Spirit said when she came back into the dining hall, "I like a man with initiative."

Astro laughed. "I'm glad, but that still doesn't make me a good candidate for you."

She laughed as well. "Maybe not, but it makes it easier for us to work together. Let's go. I want to get out on the lake."

Each of them shouldering a bag, they headed down the road to Sailor Bay, the unit closest to the lake. Another five minutes brought them to the cove where the camp's boats were moored. "I thought we'd take the Hunter 140," Spirit said. "It's got a little more space, since we have the gear, but we can still beach it rather than having to leave it at anchor and swim to shore or find a dock."

"Sounds good to me," Astro said, settling a PFD over his shoulders and making sure it fit correctly. "I'm sure a swim will feel good at some point today, but I'm not sure I want to set up camp soaking wet."

Spirit laughed. "You mean getting rained on at the campout was enough?"

"It was an eye-opening experience," Astro said. "Let's leave it at that." The memory of seeing C.C. in the tent as he changed clothes flashed back through Astro's mind, but he pushed it aside as they rigged the boat and set the sail. Spirit sealed the dry bags and secured them so they wouldn't fall out of the boat even if it capsized. The cove was protected enough not to permit a lot of speed, but once they were out onto the main body of the lake, the wind and waves picked up, not enough to rock the boat dangerously, but definitely enough to intensify the experience. Spirit handled the lines with quiet competence, reminding him again of how long she'd been a part of this place and all it entailed.

They spent the first hour on the water reveling in the experience, Spirit pointing out various places of interest along the lake: a supposedly haunted island that was created when the dam was built to form the lake, cutting off the local cemetery from the mainland; a cove that led back toward an abandoned mine where a gruesome murder had once taken place; a promontory that overlooked the lake at the end of the local lovers' lane where more than once Spirit had caught sight of couples making out. "I've never actually caught anyone having sex," she confided, "but I suspect that's more a matter of timing."

Another half-hour passed before they reached the first of the campsites Spirit wanted to check out. They pulled up the centerboard and rudder and beached the boat, wading in to shore to check out the rocky beach and grassy area behind it. "This is why I always scope out sites before I come with the girls," she said with a grimace as she nudged at an abandoned hypodermic needle with the toe of her canvas lake shoes. Several more littered the area. "If it were just a little garbage, we'd make it a service project to clean it up, but this isn't safe. We'll have to mark this one off the list for the summer."

They went back to the boat and sailed on down the shoreline. "Do you see a lot of stuff like that?" Astro asked as they continued.

Spirit shrugged. "It varies. That beach is actually accessible by road. Not easily, but it's possible. We haven't had problems there in the past, but obviously some of the locals have started using it as a crack house. A lot of the places we camp are only accessible by boat, and that tends to make them safer. As a general rule, boaters are respectful of each other and the lake."

The next two sites they checked were pristine, reassuring Astro about the prospect of bringing campers out on the lake overnight. "If the next beach is still usable, we'll camp there for the night," Spirit said as they headed out again. "We'll need time to get a fire started and we don't want to end up eating at midnight if we can help it. We have to sail back in the morning."

"And if it isn't?" Astro asked.

"Then we'll sail back here," Spirit replied, "but I want to check all the possibilities, just in case. You never know when someone might already be using one of the coves for the night."

That made sense to Astro. They found the next cove and unpacked their gear, working in tandem to secure the boat and set up camp. They gathered firewood and started dinner, a can of soup in the bowl of each mess kit. While those were heating, they set up their tents on the grassy knoll at the top of the beach.

Once everything was settled and they started to eat, Spirit pinned Astro with a piercing look. "So what's up with you and C.C.?" she asked. "I know you're interested, and it sure looked like he was interested Thursday out at the cliff, particularly if what Limey said was true. So what's going on?"

"What did Limey say?" Astro delayed, trying to figure out how to answer Spirit's questions.

"That C.C. couldn't keep his hands to himself," Spirit replied. "She said you ignored him for the most part but that C.C. was pretty obvious, at least to anyone paying attention."

"The girls didn't notice, did they?" Astro asked, panicked.

Spirit shook her head. "The vast majority of them aren't thinking in those terms yet. And even the ones who might be thinking about boys aren't at the point of thinking about boys with other boys. Pluto agreed that you did your job despite C.C.'s attempts at distraction. Now, you didn't answer my question."

"Nothing's going on," Astro insisted. "Yeah, I'm attracted to him and I guess his antics on Thursday mean he's attracted to me, but I came to Laguna to get away from any entanglements, not get involved with new ones."

"He's an entanglement, is he?" Spirit challenged. "He doesn't have to be."

Astro sighed. "Camp will end, and where does that leave us? Even if he were willing and able to live up to my expectations as far as monogamy is concerned, we have all of seven weeks left together."

"I thought you were both at UNC-Asheville?" Spirit verified.

"He's taken some classes there, I think, enough to be familiar with the campus," Astro agreed, "but he's actually enrolled at the University of Washington."

"You're still in the same city," she pointed out. "Yes, camp friendships sometimes end with the summer, but they don't have to, Astro. Have you looked at Ricki, Yogurt, Rambler, Seuss, and me? We don't live in the same towns or go to the same schools, but we've managed to stay friends for fifteen years now. And yes, friendships survive separation easier than romances do, but we're still proof that relationships started at camp don't have to end when the summer does. I'm not saying you should start something with C.C. without considering everything, but I'm not sure the end of summer is enough of a reason not to see what develops, especially when you go to school in the same city."

"That doesn't change the fact that he's a player and I'm not," Astro reminded her. "He's out at a bar trolling again tonight. He asked me to go along. I told him I already had plans."

"You could've gone," Spirit told him. "I'd have found someone else to go with me, or I could've come alone."

Astro shook his head. "When I say I'm going to do something, I do it," he insisted. "And I wouldn't be at all comfortable with the idea of you out here by yourself. Besides, going with him and watching him pick up some other guy is hardly my idea of a good time."

"And if his plan was to pick *you* up at the bar?" Spirit queried.

"I don't want a blow job in a restroom stall," he explained, "and that's all I'd get at a bar."

Spirit laughed. "Maybe at the bar itself, but you share a tent, just the two of you. I'm pretty sure you could have more than a blow job if that's what you wanted."

"That's just it," Astro said. "It isn't what I want. I mean, I'm not opposed to the idea of sex, but fucking for the sake of fucking isn't my cup of tea. I come from an old-fashioned family. Sex is supposed to mean something."

Spirit nodded. "I understand. I really do. And it's hard to consider a new relationship when the old one is barely over."

"Exactly," Astro agreed. "If I hadn't come to Laguna until next summer, when I'd had a year to get over Jarrett, things might've been different, or if C.C. weren't such a player, but it just isn't meant to be this year. However much I might wish otherwise."

Spirit didn't seem to have an answer, reaching for the box of cookies and offering him one instead of pushing the conversation. As darkness fell, they put out the fire and retired to their tents. As Astro lay on his bedroll listening to the waves lapping at the shore, he wondered where C.C. was, and what—or who—he was doing. The thought followed him into his dreams.

CHAPTER 9

THE flap to Astro's tent opened, the zipper hissing softly as C.C. pulled aside the nylon and slipped inside. His finger went immediately to Astro's lips, silencing any questions or protests as he closed the flap behind him, cocooning them in the heated darkness of the small space. Slowly, he undressed, visible the way people are in dreams, even when the darkness should be complete, so that Astro could see every line of hard, trim muscle as C.C. disrobed. He could feel the glitter of the other man's lusty gaze on his skin, as potent as any caress. C.C. peeled away the sleeping bag covering Astro's body—his mysteriously naked body— and slid upward until their mouths met. Astro groaned softly into the kiss, arching into the delicious pleasure of skin against skin as C.C. shifted, deliberately grinding their bodies together.

Astro slid his hands down C.C.'s back, clenching tightly into bunching muscles until he reached the perfect curve of the blond's ass. He'd dreamt of getting his hands on it from the first time he saw it, and now he finally had his chance. He stroked the smooth skin, learning the feel with his palms and fingertips, relishing the opportunity to touch and arouse. C.C. wasn't idle, either, licking his way down Astro's neck to his nipples, the little points hard with desire, standing up tightly in search of more attention.

In encouragement, Astro slid his fingers between C.C.'s tight cheeks, seeking his target with unerring accuracy, fingers slipping with dreamer's ease into the snug space. C.C. bucked beneath his fingering, grinding their cocks together as his back arched. Astro took advantage, sliding lower to get his mouth on the cock bobbing in front against his belly. His fingers drove deeper, working fast and hard to bring C.C. pleasure. He could taste the cream seeping from the tip of C.C.'s cock and he lapped at it enthusiastically, wringing more moans from the man above him.

When C.C. pulled away and grabbed Astro's cock, lifting into position so he could sink down onto it, engulfing Astro in his burning passage, Astro thought he'd died and gone to heaven. He thrust up without hesitation, not even giving C.C. a chance to adjust to his girth, but if C.C.'s cries of pleasure were anything to go by, he didn't need it. Their bodies moved together in concert, the rhythm too easy to be new to either of them, pushing them quickly toward the precipice and over into rapture.

They soared together in the blissful aftermath, coming down slowly to snuggle together in Astro's sleeping bag. Astro couldn't make out the words C.C. mumbled as he fell asleep, but he heard the affection in the other man's tone and knew everything was right in the world.

The sound of an outboard motor on a fishing boat roused Astro from his dream. He scowled as he felt the sticky mess in his briefs. He hadn't had this many wet dreams since he hit puberty, but C.C. seemed to haunt him at night, each dream more vivid, more alluring than the last. Fishing around until he found his swim trunks, he changed out of his soiled underwear. He'd take a short dip in the lake. The cold water could douse his ardor and erase the evidence of last night's dreams at the same time. And maybe he'd even get dried off before Spirit woke up and he wouldn't have to explain his sudden urge for an early morning swim.

Almost as soon as he finished cleaning himself up and settled in for an actual swim, Spirit's tent opened as well and she appeared with her bathing suit on, towel in hand. "Are you sure you're gay?" she teased as she walked down the beach. "Because, I swear, you're a man after my own heart."

"Sorry," he said with an unrepentant grin. "I can appreciate female beauty with the same eye I appreciate a painting or a beautiful view, but it doesn't do anything for me on a physical level."

"Well, damn," she joked, dropping her towel next to his and joining him in the water. "I guess I'll have to settle for being your fag hag and setting you up with every gay guy I know."

The comment surprised a laugh out of him. "As long as they're interested in something beyond getting me in bed, I can probably live with that," he said, pushing aside memories of the previous night's dream. In his dreams, no matter how sexual, he always knew C.C. wanted more than merely his body.

"You have to promise to send any straight guys in my direction, though," she said, splashing him playfully before diving beneath the waist-deep water and stretching out in long, easy strokes.

"The guy who cheated on you was an idiot," Astro muttered beneath his breath as he watched her swim. If she heard him, she didn't reply, but then he hadn't been looking for one. Leaving her to her exercise, he waded back to shore, toweling off and clearing out the fire circle they'd made the night before so he could start heating water for oatmeal and tea. He'd seen Spirit with her cup of hot tea every morning and figured she'd appreciate it this morning as well. Fifteen minutes later, she joined him on the beach, her towel wrapped around her waist as they poured hot water over the instant breakfast and ate.

"It's early enough that we could probably explore a little more of the lake before we head back if you'd like," she offered when they'd finished eating and were tearing down their campsite.

Astro shook his head. "No, I think I'd rather we head back. As refreshing as the swim was, I need a real shower before the next group of campers arrives, and fitting one in is sometimes a challenge for me."

Spirit laughed. "Do we hog the showers that badly?"

"Not really," Astro said, "but there are a lot of you and the showers only hold two at a time. Which adds up to not a lot of time for me, particularly if I don't want to share a shower with C.C."

"Yeah, I can see that being tough," she agreed, checking one last time to make sure the fire was completely out. "We'll take the direct route back then."

They loaded the boat and headed back toward camp, reaching Sailor's Bay Cove in about half the time it had taken them the day before. The wind was strong without being gusty, and they flew across the waves, making Astro hope for some time this week to go sailing with Spirit's girls.

Astro found the showers empty when they got back to camp. Spirit insisted he go ahead and shower first, reminding him she could shower with any of the others later. Twenty minutes later, feeling clean and refreshed, ready for a new week and a new group of girls, Astro came face to face with C.C., looking only marginally better than he had the week before. His eyes were puffy and red-rimmed, and he looked more than a little green around the gills. "The shower's empty if you want to get cleaned up before Scruffy sees you looking like that," he offered neutrally.

"Fuck off," C.C. muttered, brushing past Astro without another word.

Astro's eyes widened as he stared after his tentmate in shock. He had no idea what had crawled up C.C.'s ass, but the other guy had another thing coming if he thought Astro would put up with that kind of attitude for long. Chalking it up to a hangover and not anything more serious, Astro walked back to the dining hall, where the staff was slowly gathering as they came back from however they'd spent their day off, but if C.C. continued with that kind of nastiness, Astro intended to set him straight, and soon.

After lunch, Scruffy gave them their assignments for the afternoon, sending Astro to the infirmary station with C.C. to do the health checks for the incoming campers. Astro's stomach dropped at the thought. After the run-in they'd had that morning, the last thing Astro wanted was to be cooped up with C.C. all afternoon, unable to clear the air between them because of the campers and parents looking on.

C.C. looked better than he had that morning, the pallor gone from his skin. If Astro looked closely, which he refused to admit he was doing, he could still see a trace of redness around C.C.'s eyes, a little bit of a pinch around his lips, but for the most part, he looked his usual, sober self. The first wave of campers arrived before they could even get everything set up. They fumbled through finding registration cards, checking health information, taking vitals and searching for lice and athlete's foot, getting the girls processed in an almost reasonable amount of time.

They spent their first respite getting everything organized so they would be better prepared to deal with the next wave, which arrived almost as soon as they had everything they needed in place. Astro was quietly grateful for being so busy. He didn't want to hear about C.C.'s conquest the night before.

Thirty minutes later, they experienced another lull in the flow of newcomers. Astro slumped into the seat usually occupied by one of the campers.

"Long night?" C.C. drawled the moment Astro was settled.

"Not particularly," Astro replied coolly, already not liking the tone of the conversation.

"Don't tell me Spirit was disappointing," C.C. jeered.

Astro scowled. "You know it was just a sailing trip. She's a lovely woman, but I'm not interested in her."

"You couldn't prove it by me," C.C. retorted.

Astro's reply was cut off by the arrival of two more campers. He bit his tongue as they took care of the girls, but as soon as they were alone, Astro rounded on C.C. "At least I have the good sense not to get drunk off my ass and pick up some random guy in a bar."

C.C. snorted. "You're just angry that I got some last night and you didn't."

Astro rolled his eyes. "A minute ago, you were accusing me of sleeping with Spirit. Make up your mind."

"You're jealous."

"Of a blow job in a bar restroom?" Astro scoffed. "Dream on. I like to know a guy's name before I stick my dick in his mouth. It means more that way."

Three more campers arrived, forestalling C.C.'s reply. When they had left, C.C. crowded him against the wall. "You know my name."

"Is that an invitation?" Astro demanded, the words out before he could censor them.

"Name the time and place," C.C. said immediately.

"Tonight in the showers, after lights out," Astro said, his anger silencing all the reasons why this was a bad idea.

"Done," C.C. said, glaring at him.

They didn't have another private moment during registration.

Astro pointedly ignored C.C. during dinner and the opening campfire and its aftermath, accepting Yogurt's invitation to join her girls for some songs and S'mores rather than going back to his tent and having to face C.C.

Finally, Yogurt sent her little girls off to bed, and Astro had no more excuses to delay. With heavy feet, he trudged toward the staff house. He'd challenged C.C. that afternoon in the heat of anger, but his dream from the night before kept haunting him. If he and C.C. were lovers, he'd take a blow job in the shower in a heartbeat, but they weren't. This encounter would be the same kind of meaningless fling he'd jeered at C.C. for having the night before. The thought turned his stomach, but he didn't know how to get out of it. He'd issued the challenge, not C.C.

Spirit was sitting on the porch of the staff house when he arrived. "I thought you'd be out in your unit with your girls," he said as he sat down beside her.

"Patches and Captain can handle a campfire by themselves," Spirit said with a half-smile. "They've been here almost as long as I have. I wasn't in the mood for the laughter and singing tonight."

Astro's eyes widened. Spirit, of the "Have Song, Will Sing" award, not in the mood for music? "What's wrong?"

She shrugged. "Nothing that time won't solve," she promised. "Gene and I broke up a month ago tonight. I'm just feeling a little down, that's all, and I didn't want to inflict that on the girls their first night at camp. I'll be fine in the morning."

Astro wasn't sure how true that was, but he let it go.

"So how was your day?" she asked before he could say anything else. "Did you survive working with C.C. all afternoon?"

Astro squirmed uncomfortably. "Yeah, although I think I did something stupid."

Spirit raised an eyebrow. "Yes?" she prompted when he didn't go on.

"I sort of challenged him to give me a blow job," Astro muttered.

"You did what? Astro, you spent all of yesterday telling me you didn't want a meaningless fling."

"I know," Astro groaned. "I didn't mean to do it. It just came out. He was jeering at me for going sailing with you, implying it was more than a camping trip. I couldn't help myself. I told him I liked to know a guy's name before I let him suck me off. The next thing I know, he's challenging me to name a time and place, given that I know *his* name. It was stupid. I know it was stupid. But I was angry and horny and he was offering and…."

"When is this supposed to happen?" Spirit asked disapprovingly.

"More or less now," Astro answered, hanging his head. "After lights out, in the showers."

"You realize this isn't even about sex at all," she told him. "You've started a pissing match over something absolutely ridiculous and it's going to keep degenerating if you let it start."

"I know," Astro groaned. "I really do."

Spirit stood up. "My break's almost over and I've got to get back. Think about this, though. You have to work with him—not to mention live with him—for the rest of the summer. If it's going to be a casual fuck that ends up creating tension between you, you'd be better off not even letting it begin. We can't afford to have that kind of dissension given the size of the staff."

"I don't want it to be that way," Astro assured her. "I'd much prefer an actual relationship, one that has a chance of surviving the summer, but I'm afraid that won't happen."

"It certainly won't if you start it this way," Spirit reminded him. "If it's worth having, it's worth waiting for. C.C. isn't a bad guy and he really has grown up a lot since last summer. Try making it clear to him what you want from him, and what you need to go forward. He might surprise you."

Astro nodded as she walked away, the gravel crunching beneath her boots. Sitting on the porch in silence, the faint light of the moon silvering the lawn in front of the staff house, Astro sought the same sense of peace he'd felt on Friday night after the closing campfire, but it proved elusive, his upcoming confrontation with C.C. keeping him from relaxing in the quiet darkness.

He could stay and let C.C. blow him and keep his pride for tonight, but he'd lose all his self-respect in the morning. And he'd prove to C.C. that all his comments about meaningless encounters were really a bunch of lies. Or he could stick to his principles and tell C.C. he didn't want the blow job after all. That would be a lie as well, but at least it would be one that wouldn't hurt anyone except himself. It might scuttle his chances of having a relationship with C.C. later, but he was pretty sure a meaningless blow job now would guarantee he'd never have that relationship.

With a groan, he thumped his head against the headrest of the chair. Once again, his big mouth had gotten him in trouble. One of these days, he'd learn to keep his trap shut until he could think through what he was about to say. Today hadn't been that day, though, and now he had to figure out how to get out of this mess without making things worse. Spirit had suggested telling C.C. the truth, but Astro wasn't sure he was ready to do that, especially not if C.C. was still in the confrontational mood from that afternoon. Heart-to-hearts were hard enough when both people involved wanted to have one. When one of them—or both of them, if Astro was honest—wasn't in the mood, they were nearly impossible.

Rising to his feet, Astro decided to avoid another confrontation tonight if he could. He'd let his absence speak for him and try to talk to C.C. rationally tomorrow or the next day, when they'd both calmed down.

His plan might have worked if he'd come to his decision five minutes earlier, but C.C. stepped off the road onto the lawn at the same time Astro descended the porch steps.

"Chickening out?" C.C. demanded as Astro walked toward him, away from the staff house and showers.

"No," Astro replied honestly, "but I don't want to be another notch on your bedpost. I'd rather still respect myself in the morning."

He didn't give C.C. a chance to reply, brushing past him—and ignoring the tingle of desire that sparked along his nerves at the fleeting contact—and going back to the tent. He didn't think C.C. would press the issue, but if he did, Astro would take his mattress and bedroll and sleep in the trail house for tonight. He didn't trust himself not to give in otherwise.

Chapter 10

C.C. hadn't said anything to Astro on Sunday night when he came back to the tent after the aborted blow job. In the intervening days, they'd managed to avoid each other almost completely, sitting on opposite sides of the dining hall at meal times and choosing to be different places when they had free time and a choice of how to fill it.

It wasn't really what Astro wanted, but he couldn't figure out a way to break the ice without starting another argument and he didn't want to do that. He wanted to go back to Sunday and avoid the entire conversation that had landed them in this mess to begin with, but since that wasn't possible, he'd bide his time until the weekend and try to talk to C.C. then. At least then they could have the conversation without an audience of campers.

They'd separated back into units for evening activities when Scruffy came running into Pine Grove, where Astro was helping Yogurt's girls with basic knot tying. "Storm's coming," he said urgently. "Get the girls to the dining hall and then come back to secure your unit if you can."

"A storm?" Astro asked.

Yogurt calmly told the girls to gather their ropes and take them up to the dining hall. The light would be better up there, she explained.

The girls seemed to pick up on the tension among the counselors, glancing around warily as they followed Yogurt's directions. Scruffy had already left, running full tilt toward the outlying units. "Do I need to head toward Bob White?" Astro asked Yogurt softly.

Yogurt shook her head. "Brook will let them know and she'll get to TIC Hollow as well. Scruffy hits Pine Grove on his way out to Redwood and Sailor Bay. Let's get the girls settled and then we'll see what's what. We all have radios for emergencies, but when the storms roll in, the reception often gets too bad for them to do any good."

Astro nodded, following at the end of the line of girls as Yogurt and her staff led the way to the dining hall. The wind had already picked up, the sky darkening quickly as heavy clouds obscured the setting sun. By the time they reached the dining hall, large drops of rain had started to fall, stinging their bare skin as they were whipped about by the ever-increasing wind.

Yogurt sent Birdie and Pluto, her assistants that week, inside with the girls while she and Astro closed the wooden shutters on all the windows. If the storm got as bad as it threatened to, they'd be glad of the extra layer of protection. By the time they'd secured the shutters, they were both soaked to the skin. "I've got to check the tents," Yogurt told Astro. "Can you head to the staff house to make sure everything is secure up there?"

"Will you be all right alone?" Astro asked, not sure he wanted anyone unaccounted for in the worsening storm.

"I won't be alone," Yogurt assured him as Ricki and Rambler appeared with their girls. "We'll go together to each of the units, and we won't take any chances. If things get too bad, we'll come back here or take shelter in the CIT hut in TIC Hollow. Don't feel like you have to make it back to the dining hall. You can stay in the staff house until the storm passes if you need to."

C.C. ran up, joining the other staff members. "Spirit and Seuss are safe in the arts and crafts house with Loopy, Ginger, and the twins. Has anyone made it to the staff house?"

"Astro's going that way now," Yogurt said. "Go with him. We shouldn't have anyone out alone if we can help it."

Astro wanted to protest, to suggest that C.C. go with her and one of the Amazons come with him, but the three women had already raced off toward Bob White, leaving C.C. with him. "Let's go," he said tersely.

They ran up the road as fast as they could in the buffeting wind, the force of the gusts nearly knocking Astro off his feet more than once. C.C. caught him before he could fall, steadying him and helping him on. Astro returned the favor a few seconds later when C.C. stumbled.

Finally, they reached the porch of the staff house. The wind continued to drive the rain against them, though they couldn't get any more soaked. Astro fumbled with the shutters on the front porch while C.C. went around to the side, closing those shutters as well.

Shivering as the temperature dropped along with the blinding rain, Astro pulled the door open, bracing it against the wind as C.C. joined him. The wind tore it from their grasp, slamming it shut behind them as they stumbled across the threshold, dripping water in their wake.

"Are there any rags?" Astro asked C.C., trying to keep his voice even despite his pounding heart. "There's water all over the floor from the windows and we're only adding to it."

"There should be some under the sink by the water heater," C.C. replied breathlessly as thunder clapped loudly overhead. The lights flickered momentarily before coming back on. Even with the shutters closed, Astro could feel the chill in the room. He went into the mudroom that led to the outdoor showers and checked under the sink, finding a bucket full of rags. He carried them back into the main room, his breath catching in his throat as C.C. stripped the sopping T-shirt over his head. He told himself the other man wasn't putting on a show for him as he toweled dry, but he couldn't stop the little gasp that escaped him when C.C. reached for the snap on his shorts.

"See something you like?" C.C. drawled, glancing over his shoulder as he pushed his shorts and boxers all the way off and rubbed the chill-pinkened skin dry.

"Yeah," Astro admitted, "but you already knew that."

"Did I?" C.C. asked, wrapping the towel around his waist as he turned and stalked past Astro to get the set of clean clothes he kept at the staff house for emergencies. "I thought maybe I did, but you sure as hell didn't act like it on Sunday."

"I don't want a summer fling, all right?" Astro snapped. "And nothing you've said or done since we've been here suggests you'd be interested in anything else. I'm not asking for a promise of forever, but I don't want to start something that I already know will end when camp does. My heart doesn't work that way."

"Why should I act interested in something that wasn't on the table?" C.C. retorted, pulling on dry boxers and a T-shirt. "Hell, I didn't even know *you* were on the table until a week ago, and I wasn't going to pass up a round of hot sex for a pipe dream."

"You knew I was gay when you went out last weekend," Astro insisted.

"I did," C.C. said, "but you blew me off when I invited you to go out with me."

"You didn't ask me out," Astro shouted. "You invited me to tag along while you went trolling. There is a difference, you know."

"No," C.C. insisted, "I asked you out."

"You said, and I quote, 'I know a bar where we can get some action.' I don't call that a date," Astro said, glaring at him.

"I also said no one would look at us sideways," C.C. said quietly.

"Whatever," Astro spat, throwing the rags on the floor by the windows where they could soak up the water. "I'm going back to the dining hall."

He'd barely crossed the threshold when hard hands grabbed his shoulders, pulling him back inside at the same moment that lightning struck the old pine tree not ten feet from the door of the staff house. "Like hell you are," C.C. growled, pressing Astro hard against the wooden door, their lips colliding fiercely.

The random thought that they should make sure the lightning strike hadn't started a forest fire flitted through Astro's mind, disappearing the moment C.C.'s lips closed over his. They were hot, moving against his with determined force, daring him to ignore what was happening between them, challenging him to respond. With a hoarse groan, he gave up the internal fight and relaxed into the kiss, lips parting in eager welcome. C.C.'s tongue surged into Astro's mouth, finding his, electricity sparking between them with all the power of the storm that continued to rage unheeded outside.

C.C.'s hands moved demandingly over Astro's wet clothes, pushing them out of the way in his search for skin. Astro shook his head in protest. He couldn't—wouldn't—stop the kiss, but he wasn't ready for more than that, not without establishing some parameters first. C.C. soothed Astro with a murmur, his hands leaving the soaked cotton and moving to cradle Astro's face instead, running his fingers through Astro's short hair. Astro could definitely live with that. He slumped against the door, bringing his mouth more in line with C.C.'s and beginning his own exploration of the other man's mouth.

C.C. tasted of sugar, making Astro wonder if he'd been eating S'mores with one of the units when the storm blew in. Hungrily, he chased every last hint of flavor in C.C.'s mouth, eliciting a deep groan from the object of his attentions. Lifting his head slightly, he met C.C.'s blue eyes, searching for a sign his tentmate felt something other than simple lust for him.

The lights flickered again, not coming back on this time, leaving them shrouded in darkness. "Well, damn," C.C. muttered. "And I bet you don't have a flashlight."

Astro grinned, though he knew C.C. couldn't see it in the pitch black. "Actually, I do. I started keeping one here in the staff house on the theory I could get up here on the road even in the middle of the night if I needed to. Aren't you glad I planned ahead?"

"Get the damn thing and quit smirking," C.C. grumbled, backing away enough to let Astro move. As Astro went to rummage in his cubby for his spare flashlight, he heard C.C. grousing about his dry clothes being all wet again.

"You knew I was still soaked when you pushed me up against the door," Astro reminded C.C., flipping on the flashlight. The beam barely penetrated the inky darkness, casting shadows across C.C.'s face.

"Yeah, well, let's just say I wasn't thinking straight," C.C. said. "You'd just tried to walk out into a raging storm and nearly got hit by lightning. I wasn't about to let you go a second time."

The words brought a genuine smile to Astro's face. "I honestly wasn't sure you cared," he admitted softly. "I know you've got to think I'm blowing hot and cold on you, but I had a relationship end rather abruptly when the guy I trusted proved himself totally unreliable by sleeping around behind my back. It's left me rather wary about anything casual or anyone who takes sex casually. It doesn't make you less attractive, though, and that dichotomy is driving me crazy."

"Who uses words like dichotomy?" C.C. teased, coming to Astro's side and stroking his cheek gently to soften the gibe.

Astro shrugged. "I like words. Sue me."

C.C. shook his head. "I'd much rather kiss you again, if it's all the same to you."

Astro hesitated.

"Look, Astro," C.C. said, taking Astro's hand and pulling him close again. "I don't know what the end of the summer will bring, but if we're together, we're together. I won't play around, and not because there aren't any other interesting guys at camp this summer. I like sex. I don't mind casual sex. But I'm not going to mess up a good thing for no reason. And if you and me together stops being a good thing, I have enough respect for myself—not to mention for you—to tell you that and end things before I go back to casual sex. Now, can I please kiss you again?"

Astro had nodded his permission before the words even sank in. C.C.'s lips took his again and that made thinking pretty much irrelevant. Where their first kiss had been all lust and adrenaline and heart-pounding fear, the second one was soft and sweet and full of tenderness and affection, exactly what Astro needed and had feared he wouldn't find with the apparently footloose C.C.

"You're still soaked through," C.C. murmured when they came up for air. "Take your T-shirt off. You'll catch a chill sitting around in wet clothes."

"You just want to get me undressed," Astro teased back as C.C. pulled away to get Astro's towel.

C.C. shook his head as he returned, draping the cloth over Astro's shoulders. "I won't say no to getting naked with you at some point," he assured Astro, "but at the moment, getting us both warm and dry is far more important. We have no idea how long this storm is going to last. I'd suggest we think about getting a fire going so we have some warmth through the night."

Astro saw the logic in that. The wind had died down a little, but the rain still drummed heavily on the roof and he could see the flashes of lightning around the edges of the closed shutters. Even with everything battened down, cool air seeped in, raising goose bumps on his damp skin. "We can hang the wet clothes near the fire. They might dry faster that way."

C.C. nodded. "Come shine your flashlight over here so I can see what I'm doing. Once we get the fire going, you can check in the closets and see if there are any blankets. I'm drier than you are and I'm cold, so I know you've got to be freezing."

"I'm not too cold," Astro assured him, shining the light on the wood pile. "You warmed me up pretty well."

C.C. laughed and leered at Astro, his expression breaking into a grin. "That won't last long." He pulled out the wood he wanted, putting it in the stone fireplace and setting match to tinder. Before long, he had a merry blaze going. "See if you can find a blanket or two."

Astro rummaged through the storage closets, finally coming up with one dusty blanket. He came back to C.C. with his prize. "We'll have to share, but it's better than nothing," he said, shaking out the heavy cover.

C.C. glanced up. "Good. Get rid of your wet shorts, too, or the blanket won't help us much. You can leave your underwear on. I'm sure they're wet, but it'll be hard enough keeping my hands to myself with them on. I don't trust myself to be good if you take them off too."

Astro let out the breath he didn't know he'd been holding. He could feel his shivers intensifying and knew they needed to get dry and warm as quickly as possible so they didn't fall sick, but he'd been worried C.C. would try to take advantage of the situation. He only had the other man's word that he wouldn't, but he wanted to trust that. He *needed* to trust that, so he'd take the chance and deal with his own bit of temptation as C.C. snuggled up against him beneath the blanket.

He stripped off his shorts, toweling his legs dry and using the cloth to get as much water out of his briefs as possible. They'd hide even less than usual, wet as they were, but it wasn't like C.C. hadn't already seen him naked. He debated for a moment, and then grabbed one of the other towels off the rack. He'd apologize to whoever he'd borrowed from in the morning, but he didn't want to sit directly on the couch with wet clothes. Tossing it over the cushions, he pulled the sofa closer to the fireplace, sitting down on it and pulling the blanket over him. A few moments later, C.C. rose from his crouch by the fireplace. He smiled at Astro as he pulled off his second T-shirt and spread all of their wet clothes out on the hearth to dry.

Astro bit his lip to keep from moaning at the sight of all that tanned skin limned by the firelight. He had no idea how he was supposed to not touch when C.C. joined him under the blanket. When C.C. turned back to him, Astro caught sight of his pink nipples, taut from the cold, and lost the battle to silence any sounds of desire.

"I thought we were behaving ourselves," C.C. teased as he sat on the couch next to Astro. "Do I need to go back over by the fire instead of sharing the blanket with you?"

"No," Astro said with a shake of his head. "Neither of us will warm up as quickly that way. I'll be good, but don't ask me not to dream."

"Baby, I've been dreaming since the moment I laid eyes on you," C.C. admitted.

Astro grimaced. "Don't call me that, please. That's what Jarrett called me. Anything but that."

"Sorry, Astro," C.C. apologized immediately. "I didn't know."

"I know you didn't." Astro, lifted the edge of the blanket and invited C.C. to move closer. "The thing is, most of the memories are good ones. All except listening to him calling me that as he tried to explain why he was in bed with another guy."

C.C. flinched. "Yeah, I can see that being off-putting. I'll come up with something else to call you when we're alone. Later." Not waiting for Astro's reply, he slid his arms around Astro's torso, fitting their bodies together beneath the blanket to conserve body heat.

Astro leaned into the embrace, nuzzling C.C.'s jaw. "You realize that we'll never live it down if the rest of the staff comes looking for us and finds us like this."

C.C. smiled. "It's still raining. The wind's quieted down a little, but they aren't going to get soaked when they know we're up here at the staff house."

"They don't know for sure we made it up here," Astro reminded him.

C.C. shook his head. "The Amazons assume everyone is as competent as they are. As long as they made it back to the dining hall after securing the units, they'll assume we made it up here and got everything secured as well. Nobody will come looking for us before morning."

"Not helping me be good," Astro muttered.

C.C. laughed and kissed Astro lightly. "So we'll talk about something else. Tell me about your classes. You didn't talk much about yourself the night we all went out to dinner except to say you were at UNC-A."

"I'm studying forestry," Astro said. "It's a relatively new program on campus, but Asheville's the perfect place for it, with the mountains literally right there. I can be on the Blue Ridge Parkway in twenty minutes, thirty if traffic is bad."

C.C. nodded. "Then this is the perfect job for you. It gets you out in the woods all summer long."

Astro smiled. "That was a side benefit, for sure. The real reason I thought it was the perfect job was because it's a girls' camp. No distractions, no temptations, no one to bother me while I licked my wounds."

"Sorry about that," C.C. said, though he didn't sound sorry at all.

"I'm not," Astro said. "I didn't come here looking for anything except a way to spend the summer, but I'm not going to complain about what I found."

"Good," C.C. said with a grin, snuggling closer to Astro. "We should probably try to get some sleep if we can."

Astro couldn't believe he wanted to disagree, but with C.C. warm and nearly naked against him, memories of his dream the night before, and the one before that, and the one before that, came rushing back. His fingers itched to explore as they had done so many times as he slept, but he held back. If C.C. could restrain himself, Astro would as well. He was quite sure they'd end up in bed before long, but as they warmed up beneath the blanket, he relaxed into the comfort of holding and being held, and found that he didn't mind waiting after all.

Chapter II

"SO WHERE are you planning on spending cooks' night out?" C.C. asked Astro the next morning as they walked back toward their tent. All around them, they saw evidence of the night's storm. Branches littered the road and leaves were scattered everywhere, but the air smelled fresh, like the maelstrom of the night before had washed away all that came before. Astro smiled at his own foolishness, but foolish or not, the sentiment certainly seemed to apply to his relationship with C.C. A different man walked beside him now than the one he'd thought he knew. Gone was the devil-may-care playboy and in his place was a considerate lover.

They had cuddled close all night, C.C. getting up several times to add wood to the fire. Astro had offered to do it as well, but each time, C.C. insisted Astro was colder than he was and should stay beneath the blanket where it was warm. Astro felt guilty letting C.C. do all the work, but his tentmate was adamant. Eventually Astro gave in, feeling it would be churlish to keep arguing.

Astro smiled as he answered C.C.'s question. "With Spirit, of course." When C.C. scowled at that, Astro glanced around quickly to make sure they were alone before leaning over and kissing C.C. sweetly. "You know I'm not interested in her," he reminded the blond. "If I were, I wouldn't have been with you last night."

"I know," C.C. grumbled, "but you don't have to be quite so friendly with her."

"Yes, I do," Astro disagreed, "but you're welcome to come with me to make sure I behave myself."

"Don't think I won't!" C.C. retorted. "I don't want her thinking I can't take care of my man."

Astro laughed joyously.

"You're in a good mood this morning," Ricki called as she came up into the road, heading for the staff house.

"I sure am," Astro said, not seeing any reason to elaborate beyond that.

"Good," Ricki said. "We were getting worried about your long face."

"All gone," Astro said. "Just smiles from now on." As Ricki walked on up the road, Astro winked at C.C. "Right?"

"Absolutely," C.C. agreed.

T H E day passed quickly for Astro, even though he only caught sight of C.C. momentarily at lunchtime. He finished early with his afternoon rappelling group because Seuss wanted plenty of time to cook so dinner would be ready at a reasonable hour. Astro was in the trail house storing the last of the ropes when arms wrapped around him from behind.

"Have a good day?" C.C.'s voice murmured in his ear.

Astro smiled, turning in C.C.'s embrace. "A very good day." He dropped a quick kiss on the smiling lips that met his eagerly, not knowing how long their privacy would last. Most of the girls were already in their units preparing dinner, but that didn't mean all the support staff was likewise engaged, and Astro wasn't ready to share his new relationship with everyone just yet.

"So what's Spirit having for dinner?" C.C. asked.

"I think she said something about stir-fried rice and curry chicken."

"I have to give her one thing," C.C. commented as they walked back toward their tent. "The woman can cook."

"Good," Astro said, "because I'm hungry!"

They picked up jackets, their mess kits, and flashlights before starting the hike out to Sailor Bay. When they got there, one group of girls already had the campfire going while another group worked on preparations for dinner.

"So are you going to tell us what C.C. stands for this year?" Max, one of the older campers, asked almost as soon as Astro and C.C. joined them in the unit shelter.

"Nope," C.C. said immediately. "You have to figure it out."

"Will you tell us if we guess correctly?" Maria, another of the girls, demanded.

"Yes. If you guess it correctly, I'll tell you."

Astro snickered, wondering what the girls would come up with and what the real meaning behind the name was. Come to think of it, he didn't know C.C.'s real name, either. He'd have to ask later, when they were alone, and hope his tentmate would be more forthcoming with him than he was with the girls.

"Guess all you want," Spirit said, entering the conversation, "but don't forget to work on dinner at the same time. I'd rather not be eating at midnight if it's all the same to you."

That got the girls focused on their respective tasks again. Judging from the looks on their faces, they'd had that happen to them in previous years. "It's easy to forget exactly how long it can take to cook a meal over a campfire," Spirit explained. "If you don't start early enough or don't have a good fire going, the cooking time can stretch and stretch and suddenly it's time for lights out and you still haven't eaten, or the meat's only half-cooked. I think we've all had a disaster like that a time or two. I've learned to start early and make sure the fire is really hot."

"I'm certainly glad of your expertise," Astro said.

"Corn Cob," one of the girls said suddenly as she looked up from washing ears of corn. "That could be what C.C. stands for."

Astro glanced at C.C. who grinned, but shook his head. "Not even close."

The girls went back to muttering among themselves as they chopped vegetables.

"Crawfish Catcher."

"Yuck!" C.C. retorted immediately. "Who'd want to catch those things?"

"Any good Southern boy," Astro insisted with a grin. "They make for some seriously good eating."

C.C. shook his head adamantly. "No way. Absolutely not!"

"Don't let my mama hear you say that," Astro whispered, leaning forward to speak into C.C.'s ear as he rose and went to check on the girls supervising the campfire. Behind him, he heard Patches call out, "Cubic centimeter?"

"Geek!" C.C. replied, making her laugh. "Who knows that kind of stuff?"

"Seuss, Rambler, and anyone else entering the medical profession?" Spirit suggested.

"Patches is sixteen," C.C. protested.

"Seventeen," Patches said. "And my dad's a doctor. I know all kinds of things."

"Fine," C.C. grumbled. "And no, that isn't what it means."

Leaving the girls guessing, Spirit joined Astro by the campfire. "Cock chaser?" she whispered in his ear.

Astro spluttered out a laugh, looking up to meet Spirit's mischievous grin. "Not anymore," he answered softly. "He promised."

Spirit's eyes widened. "Stay around after lights out. I want to talk to you."

Astro nodded as Spirit called for the girls in the shelter to bring the food so they could start cooking.

An hour later, the cooks proudly served up their rice and curry, and Astro found that C.C. was correct: Spirit could cook a damn good meal on a campfire. They stayed to help supervise cleanup while Patches and Captain went to take their showers. They were back in time to relieve Spirit at lights out.

"Go away, C.C.," she ordered as the three of them started toward the staff house. "I want to talk to Astro and you're in the way."

"Spirit!" both men spluttered.

"What?" she asked. "I could beat around the bush or try to hide my intentions, but why bother? I'm going to sit in the dining hall with Astro and you, C.C., are going to go somewhere else."

"I'll go up to the staff house," C.C. said with far more aplomb than Astro could've managed if their situations were reversed. "Come find me when you're done talking?" he added for Astro alone.

"I will," Astro promised.

Spirit waited to turn on Astro until she couldn't hear C.C.'s footsteps on the gravel road anymore. "You want to tell me what's going on?" she asked. "The last time we talked, you were avoiding him because all he wanted from you was casual sex."

Astro shrugged. "So maybe he wants a little more from me than just that."

"A little more?" Spirit pressed.

"He's willing to give a relationship a try," Astro said. "And that's what I wanted all along."

"I thought you were worried about his tomcatting," she reminded him.

"I was," Astro agreed, "but as he pointed out last night, he didn't even know I was gay when we all went into Asheville together. He promised not to sleep around."

"And you believe him?" Spirit asked quietly.

"I do," Astro replied firmly. "I know, from things he's said and from other people's comments, that he wasn't exactly the perfect guy in the past, but you said yourself he'd grown up a lot."

"Because he said he was confining his sleeping around to other people who were doing the same thing, as opposed to making promises he didn't intend to keep," Spirit reminded Astro.

"I know that," Astro said earnestly, "but if he reached that point and now he's willing to make those promises, then maybe he actually means them this time."

"And if he doesn't?"

"Then you can say 'I told you so'," Astro offered.

"Like that'll make either of us feel any better," Spirit scoffed. "It's your decision to make. Just be careful when the girls are around. I don't think they picked up on the vibe tonight, but they aren't stupid, either. And you don't want the fallout of a parent complaining about public displays of affection."

Astro nodded. "I know. We'll be discreet."

"So when did this happen anyway?" Spirit asked.

"Last night during the storm," Astro admitted. "I started to charge out of the staff house and nearly got hit by lightning. C.C. grabbed me back inside and kissed me. My pounding heart didn't have anything to do with the storm."

Spirit laughed. "Well, good for him. I'm glad he's the one who started it. Maybe that means you're right after all. I hope you are. Now, he's waiting for you."

"Don't you need a shower?" Astro asked. "We can wait for you to finish."

Spirit smiled. "I took my break this morning. I'll be fine until tomorrow. And Astro, be safe as well as discreet."

Astro shook his head. "I'm not ready for anything that would require that kind of concern," he assured her. "We've kissed, that's all."

Spirit didn't have to say she didn't expect it to stay that way for long. Her expression said it for her. Astro didn't bother arguing. He and C.C. hadn't talked about the progression of their relationship, but Astro knew he didn't want to rush into anything physical. He wanted to savor the sweet cuddling like the night before for a while before they got more sexual.

"Everything okay?" C.C. asked when Astro reached the staff house.

"Everything's fine," Astro assured him, sitting down next to him on the couch where they'd slept the night before. "Spirit wanted to check on me, that's all. I spent the weekend bemoaning the fact that you were out at a bar, sleeping around, and she made me come to my senses Sunday night. She was surprised to see us together tonight and so clearly more at ease than we had been."

"You told her?" C.C. asked.

Astro nodded. "I hope you don't mind. I mean, we didn't talk about keeping it a secret from the other staff. I can try to catch her, ask her not to tell anyone else, if you want."

C.C. shook his head. "Relax," he said, rubbing Astro's shoulders lightly. "I'm not ashamed of you. We can't tell the campers, obviously, but I don't care if the Amazons know. They know all about each other's lives outside camp, so why not ours too? I didn't want to say anything if you hadn't. That's why I checked."

Astro let C.C.'s hands work their magic, resolutely not imagining them caressing other, more susceptible parts of his body. He leaned back against C.C.'s chest, relaxing fully when C.C.'s arms came around his chest, holding him lightly.

"We really should take showers and get some sleep," C.C. murmured, his breath tickling Astro's ear. "Tomorrow's Friday and it'll be a busy day for all of us."

Astro flushed, thinking about going out to the shower with C.C., watching him bathe in the diffuse light of their flashlights and the moon. His cock twitched in his shorts, eager for attention. "I'm not sure that's a good idea," he said hoarsely. "I don't trust myself to keep my hands to myself if I go out there with you. It's too soon. And—"

C.C. swallowed the rest of Astro's words in his kiss, his tongue surging deep, twining with Astro's and stealing his breath and his wits. Astro turned in C.C.'s embrace, pressing against the other man's body, determined to drive C.C. just as wild.

The sound of the door banging startled them apart. It was only the wind, but it reminded them both of where they were, and of the necessity of practicing discretion. "Go take your shower," C.C. told Astro softly, trailing his fingers down Astro's face. "I'm going to sit here and imagine you out there, naked and wet in the moonlight."

Astro groaned. "You can't say things like that and expect me to resist."

C.C. smiled and kissed Astro lightly. "Not tonight," he insisted. "I don't want you thinking I agreed to your conditions last night so I could get my hands on you tonight. I won't be able to wait long, but we're going to wait as long as we can so you don't start doubting me later."

It was the one thing C.C. could've said that would actually work. Reluctantly, Astro rose from his place in C.C.'s arms and gathered his shower bucket and towel. "Are you sure you won't join me?"

"This weekend," C.C. promised, "when there aren't any campers and most everyone else is gone."

Astro bit back another groan as he headed out the door. The water was hot, a startling contrast to the cool night air. Astro washed quickly, wishing C.C. were out there with him. The wind rustled the trees lightly, alternately veiling and revealing the stars above. His skin prickled as he turned to rinse his back, the cool breeze raising goose bumps along his chest, pebbling his nipples. He closed his eyes, imagining for a moment that C.C. was in the shower with him now, free to touch. He caught his nipples between his thumbs and forefingers, tweaking lightly, then with more enthusiasm, pretending C.C. was touching him that way instead. One hand lingered on his chest while the other slid down his abdomen to encircle his cock, stroking languidly.

"Wouldn't you rather I do that?" C.C.'s voice broke into Astro's fantasy. His eyes flew open to see his tentmate standing at the entrance to the shower enclosure.

"I thought you were going to wait inside," Astro said with a gasp, his hands dropping to his side.

"I was," C.C. replied with a shrug. "You were taking too long, and I got lonely." Tossing the towel around his waist over the aluminum wall, C.C. stalked toward Astro, his body rubbing against Astro's slick skin as his hands caught a handful of firm muscle and pulled their hips into alignment.

Astro gasped again as their hard cocks bumped, dueling with the same enthusiasm. C.C. undulated against him for a moment before spinning Astro in his arms, the water spilling over their shoulders to run down Astro's chest as C.C. pressed tightly against his back. Astro could feel C.C.'s erection nudging against his butt, seeking its place beneath the hard cheeks. Astro spread his stance a little, parting the twin globes enough for C.C.'s cock to slide between them. He moaned as C.C. bumped against him deliberately while running his hands in opposite directions over Astro's skin. One hand found the still-tight nipples Astro had been playing with earlier. The other found the heavy sac between Astro's legs, fondling it gently before sliding up to close around Astro's straining cock.

A sharp wail escaped Astro's mouth, silenced quickly by C.C.'s hand covering his. "Shhh," C.C. urged. "You have to be quiet so no one hears us."

The staff house was set well away from the rest of the camp, but even so, noises carried through the woods in the dark of night, and the last thing they wanted was someone coming to investigate.

"I'll try," Astro panted, "but it feels so good to have you touch me. I've dreamed…."

Astro could feel C.C.'s smile against his neck as the blond's hands started moving again, pulling firmly at one nipple, then the other, stroking his cock, masturbating Astro slowly, thoroughly, dare he think… lovingly. And the whole time, Astro was vividly aware of C.C.'s erection moving against his ass, rubbing up and down the channel between his cheeks. A gust of wind eddied around them, adding another layer of sensation, and Astro realized this was the single most erotic moment of his life.

"What have you dreamed?" C.C. prompted, his hands keeping their steady rhythm.

Astro bit his lip as he pressed back against C.C., trying to formulate a coherent answer to that question. "Touching you... you touching me...."

"Where are we in your dreams?" C.C. asked.

"Here in... the showers, in our... tent, in the tent from... the overnight, on the beach, at the Point..." Astro enumerated, the words coming out in sporadic bursts as C.C. continued to drive him wild.

"We'll make it to all of them," C.C. promised, his hand speeding up. "Not tonight, but before the summer's over, I'll make love to you in every single one of them."

"What if I... want to make... love to you?" Astro gasped, trying to hold back his climax a little longer.

"We can do that too," C.C. assured him. "I'm an equal opportunity lover. But right now, I want you to come for me. Show me how good it feels to have my hands on your body."

Astro gave in, sinking into C.C.'s arms as his cock sprayed all over C.C.'s hand. The steady stream of water washed away the evidence, but nothing could wash away the satisfaction he felt at the sudden rush of heat against his backside. Legs trembling with the effort to stay upright, he turned in C.C.'s arms. "I'd offer to return the favor, but...."

"Another time," C.C. promised. "For now, why don't we actually take a shower?"

Chapter 12

"And that's another group gone for the summer," C.C. said as the last parent pulled out of the parking lot and started back toward civilization. "What do you want to do with our day off?"

"Astro, C.C.!" Rambler interrupted them before Astro could reply. "We're going to camp out down at the beach. Swim, maybe take the boats out, have a big bonfire. You should join us."

Astro looked at C.C., who leaned closer and whispered, "You did mention the pup tent from the overnight. You'll have to be quiet, though, because the girls will be in the tent right next to us."

Astro's cock was hard as a rock before C.C. had even finished speaking. "Sure," he said to Rambler, trying to keep his voice steady and apparently failing miserably if the surprised look on her face was any indication.

"I don't know what you're planning," she told them, "but remember that revenge is a bitch, especially if you give Spirit reason to be in on it."

"Aw, Rambler," C.C. said, saving Astro from the awkward moment, "would we do a thing like that?"

Rambler eyed the two men suspiciously. "I don't know about Astro, but you've already proven what you're capable of. Don't think I've forgotten the shaving cream in my lake shoes."

"I keep telling you that wasn't me," C.C. insisted, turning back to wink at Astro. Astro smothered a laugh, not wanting to out his new boyfriend to Rambler if he could help it. She wasn't buying C.C.'s innocent act, though, sending him a glare that suggested she wasn't done getting her revenge yet.

They packed sandwiches for lunch and hot dogs for dinner, the Amazons insisting it was easier than lugging pots down to the beach. They spent the afternoon relaxing, frolicking in the water, having canoe races, lazing on the sailboats, and otherwise enjoying the water.

At one point, Spirit and Seuss challenged Astro and C.C. to a canoe race. Astro snorted, sure they could beat the girls hands down, but C.C. was game so they accepted the challenge.

They started side by side on the beach, racing for the canoes when Rambler shouted "Go!" Astro and C.C. got there first, though only by a few inches. That was when Astro got his first surprise. As he and C.C. fumbled with the aluminum boat, trying to get it flipped and into the water, Seuss and Spirit each grabbed an end of theirs in perfect choreography, flipping it as they ran, the paddles Astro hadn't even thought to pick up yet landing on the bottom of the canoe, easily at hand. The girls were in the water and already paddling before Astro and C.C. had gotten their canoe turned over.

"Get the paddles," C.C. shouted. "I'll drag the boat into the water."

Astro did as C.C. said, but by that point, Spirit and Seuss were already well ahead of them. They paddled as fast as they could, but they weren't used to canoeing together, so their strokes didn't match and they couldn't quite find a rhythm that worked for them.

"I give up," Astro said with a laugh as Spirit and Seuss pulled farther and farther ahead. "That'll teach me to underestimate them."

"We'll give it to them this time," C.C. said, "but we're going to practice and before the summer is over, we're going to give them a run for their money."

"You can practice your stroke with me any time you want," Astro offered.

C.C. snorted with laughter. "That wasn't the kind of practice I was thinking about, but I won't say no."

Astro grinned. "We can practice canoeing, too, but I'm not entirely sure we can beat those two. I swear, I haven't seen anything that polished outside of competitive sports."

C.C. nodded in agreement. "They've been doing it together, like everything else here at camp, for so long it's become second nature to them. But that doesn't mean we can't give them some real competition before the summer's over."

They paddled back to shore more leisurely.

"You should've come out to the lake with us last summer or the summer before," Rambler said with a shake of her head as they returned to the shore. "You'd have known better than to accept a challenge to do anything on the water from those two."

Astro chuckled. "Live and learn, I guess," he replied philosophically. "So what should I not accept *your* challenge to do?"

"Hike the Rainbow trail," Yogurt answered for Rambler. "She loves that trail—the only one of us who does, I think. So when our campers want to hike it, we switch with her for the day."

"The Rainbow trail?" Astro echoed. "That sounds right up my alley."

"Not that kind of Rainbow," C.C. joked. "The kind that comes from light shining through water droplets. It's a long, treacherous trail with nothing but ups and downs. I hiked it once. I'm not particularly eager to hike it again."

"If I'm free the next time you take a group of campers, I'll come with you," Astro offered. "I might only go once, but I'd like to see it."

"You'll regret it," C.C. muttered.

"Don't tell him that," Rambler said. "Most of the girls love that trail as much as I do."

"Nobody loves it as much as you do, Rambler," Yogurt insisted, "but you're right that the girls enjoy it far more than most of the staff. They're younger and in better shape."

Astro had to laugh at that. The idea of anyone being in better shape than the Amazons, certainly anyone who wasn't an athlete, was ludicrous. He'd spent all of staff week and the first two weeks of camp watching them run circles around everyone else.

"Hey," Ricki called. "We might want to think about getting a fire started. It's starting to get late."

Astro glanced at his watch and realized it was already seven, far later than he would've guessed. They'd only just gotten to the beach, hadn't they?

"I'll let you do that while I set up some tents," Astro said, knowing they'd get a fire going in half the time it would take him. "Give me a hand, C.C.?"

"Sure," C.C. said, grabbing one of the pup tents they'd carried down to the lake. They set up enough tents for the female staff first, all to one side of the beach.

When only their tent remained, Astro headed to the opposite end of the beach. "It's not exactly private, but it's better than being right on top of them," he murmured.

C.C. grinned at him. "Not sure you'll be able to stay quiet?"

"Not sure you'll be able to," Astro retorted. "It's my turn to get my hands on you."

With the closing campfire the night before lasting well past the usual time for lights out, and knowing they'd have to get up early in the morning and deal with parents, they'd opted for going straight to sleep instead of indulging first, leaving Astro still feeling like he'd left C.C. with the short end of the stick. He'd expected to return the favor in their tent, well away from the other staff, but he wasn't going to be deterred, regardless of the setting. He was going to get his hands on C.C.'s body. Tonight.

And if they cuddled together afterward, that would be even better.

By the time they had the tents ready, Ricki had the fire hot and everyone had come in off the lake. Astro and C.C. joined them, good-naturedly accepting the ribbing from Spirit and Seuss for losing the race.

They all gathered sticks to cook their hotdogs on, congregating around the campfire. Astro was tempted to make a comment about the relative size of everyone's sticks, but he kept it to himself. Yogurt wasn't as restrained.

"So, C.C., feeling a little... lacking in certain areas?" she teased, looking at his hotdog stick, which was at least two inches longer and significantly thicker in diameter than everyone else's.

"Not at all," C.C. said, flushing slightly in the fading light. "I simply don't want my hotdog to fall off the stick." As he spoke, the weight of Limey's hotdog defeated the strength of her stick and fell in the fire. "Like that."

Everyone hid their snickers behind their hands, but Astro could feel the mirth as Limey went in search of a new stick, a thicker one this time.

"That explains the width, but not the length," Yogurt retorted with a grin.

Astro could've told her C.C. didn't have anything to be ashamed of, but he didn't figure his boyfriend would appreciate him sharing that information with everyone else.

C.C. simply smiled enigmatically. Spirit met Astro's gaze and smirked at him, but he took his cue from C.C. and merely smiled back.

The sun set and darkness fell while they were still roasting and eating their dinner, but nobody seemed to care. The bonfire provided plenty of light. Spirit went back to her tent at Sailor Bay and got her guitar, and before long, they were all settled in the sand laughing and singing and generally enjoying the night with no campers.

Finally, everyone started drifting off toward their tents. C.C. stayed where he was, though, so Astro did the same. Eventually, even Spirit put away her guitar. "Make sure the fire's out before you go to sleep," she told them, giving them a look that suggested they not disturb anyone with their antics.

C.C. assured her they wouldn't forget and shooed her off in the direction of her tent. She rolled her eyes at him, but went as directed, ducking into the small enclosure and zipping it up behind her.

The two men sat side by side, letting the sounds of the night wash over them. Eventually, relatively sure the rest of the staff had settled down for the night, Astro scooted closer to C.C. and whispered, "If we go to our tent, I could return the favor from the other night in the showers."

C.C. smiled at him and kissed him hard. "We could do that," he agreed, "but it's an awfully small space. We could go skinny dipping in the lake. We'd have to be quiet since sound carries on the water, but we wouldn't have to worry about being cramped inside the pup tent."

Astro hesitated, glancing toward the other tents a little farther down the beach. If they swam out in the cove a bit, they wouldn't be any closer to the girls than they would be in the tent. Maybe even farther away. "All right," he said finally. "Should we put the fire out first?"

"Yeah. That way, if the girls do wake up and glance out, they'll think we've gone to bed and not go investigating any further."

They doused the fire with water, making sure all the coals were extinguished. "I don't think I've ever gone skinny dipping," Astro admitted.

C.C. laughed, smothering the sound behind his hand. "It isn't difficult," he teased. "You strip down and run in the water. When you're done, you run out and grab your towel."

Astro smacked C.C.'s arm lightly. "I know that, dolt. Let's go." He dropped his bathing suit to the sand and ran for the water, trusting C.C. would follow. When he was waist deep in the water, he turned back to watch his boyfriend sauntering toward him, giving Astro the opportunity to ogle him to his heart's content. To his delight, C.C. was already half-hard. Eventually, C.C. reached his side, the water hiding his lengthening cock. Astro pulled C.C. against him immediately, wanting to return the pleasure C.C. had lavished on him the other night. C.C. went willingly, his hands settling on Astro's hips. "You didn't actually want to swim, did you?" he asked against C.C.'s lips.

C.C. shook his head, not bothering to break the kiss to put his reply into words.

Astro slid his hands between them, seeking C.C.'s cock. He found it easily enough, bobbing in the gentle waves. His hand closed around the eager shaft, stroking hot skin and enjoying the way C.C. arched into his touch. He leaned forward, nuzzling C.C.'s neck tenderly, and let his hand start to slide in the water. C.C. might have been the one to start things between them, initiating their relationship with the incendiary kiss at the staff house on Wednesday, but Astro was determined not to be left out. He fully intended to seduce C.C. as thoroughly as he himself had been seduced. Now it was just a matter of showing those intentions to his boyfriend.

C.C. certainly seemed willing, if the way he thrust into Astro's hand was any indication, but Astro didn't want a quick, physical release. He wanted a slow seduction, the kind that said as much about their hearts as it did about their bodies. C.C. whined softly in protest when Astro slipped an arm around his hips, stilling his restless movements.

"Relax," Astro urged. "Relax and let me take care of you."

C.C. relaxed into the touch, the tension investing his limbs slowly easing as Astro continued to explore his body. The water buoyed them, relieving Astro of any worries about keeping them upright. His only concern now was how good he could make C.C. feel. His hands wandered across the broad chest he'd admired more than once, enjoying the contrast of smooth skin with his own hairier chest. When C.C. squirmed, Astro smiled and let his touch linger on the spot beneath his boyfriend's arm, stroking repeatedly until C.C. finally pulled away.

"Be careful," he warned softly. "I'm almost ticklish there."

Astro grinned. "But I like the way you squirmed when I touched you. Come back here. I won't tickle again. Or if I do, just tell me to stop."

C.C. returned to Astro's embrace, taking one of Astro's hands and guiding it back to his cock. "That's where I want your hands."

Astro blew softly in C.C.'s ear. "I'll get there; don't worry. But I want to do more than get you off. I want to savor you."

C.C. trembled in Astro's arms, making Astro wonder if anyone had ever really taken the time to linger over foreplay with C.C. He knew

C.C. wasn't averse to one-night stands and that only added to Astro's suspicions. "Let me show you how good it can be."

C.C. nodded and relaxed into Astro's arms again.

Astro took his time, his hands stroking slowly over C.C.'s skin, each caress a promise of more delights to come. C.C. writhed against him, biting his lip to keep his moans inside. Astro spun C.C. in his arms, touching his lips to the blond's. "This way, you can make all the noise you want," he whispered before capturing C.C.'s mouth in a torrid kiss.

Nothing could completely silence the moan that escaped C.C. at the suddenly passionate kiss and the more determined caress to his cock. Internally, Astro gloated at having wrung such a sound from his usually cocksure boyfriend.

A wolf whistle from the beach broke them apart, panting as they struggled to bring themselves back under control. All five Amazons sat on the beach, Seuss and Spirit twirling Astro's and C.C.'s discarded bathing suits in their hands.

"Did you lose something?" Rambler drawled.

Astro looked at C.C., then back at the Amazons. "No, I don't think anything's lost," he replied, trying to steady his voice.

"Then you won't mind coming out to claim these, will you?" Ricki challenged playfully.

Astro glanced at C.C. again.

"Come on, Rambler," C.C. pleaded. "This is way more than revenge."

"Really?" Rambler countered. "I don't think so. And the others agreed with me. Of course, we didn't expect you to make it so easy for us, either."

"I wasn't part of last summer's prank," Astro protested. "Why am I being punished too?"

"Because you took up with him," Seuss said easily. "It's guilt by association."

"That is *so* not fair," Astro grumbled.

"Deal with it," Spirit said, laughing. "You don't have anything we haven't seen before."

"Maybe," Astro said, "but you haven't seen mine before." Especially not when he was still mostly hard from his interrupted interlude with C.C. Even though he knew the water preserved his modesty, he slid his hands down over his crotch, trying to gauge whether he'd wilted enough to hide behind his palms until he could get to his towel.

"So?" Rambler challenged. "We want to see what C.C.'s getting."

"And vice versa," Yogurt added. "Come on, boys. We don't have all night."

"We could just stay here in the water until you got tired of waiting and went to bed," C.C. pointed out.

All five Amazons laughed at that. "You really think we're going to get tired before you get cold?" Rambler asked. "And even if we did, we'd just take turns sleeping. Come on, C.C. Pay up."

"This is far more than evening the odds," C.C. warned her. "If you make me come out there like this, this is war."

Spirit laughed. "Do you really want to do that?" she asked. "All five of us, and all our years of camp pranks, against you? Why would you drag poor Astro into that?"

"He didn't drag me into it," Astro retorted. "You're the one holding my shorts."

"These are yours?" Spirit verified.

Astro nodded.

She tossed them in his direction. "But if you give them to C.C. or try to help him get out of his punishment, you'll be next on our hit list."

Astro swam forward, careful to keep his lower body well beneath the water line, until he could catch his trunks. Pulling them on, he stood, returning to C.C.'s side.

"Give them what they want," he murmured in C.C.'s ear. "I'll make it up to you in our tent once they've gone back to bed."

"Easy for you to say," C.C. groused. "You're not the one who has to walk out there naked."

"Would it be easier if I walked out there with you?" Astro asked seriously.

C.C. looked at Astro in desperate relief. "Would you really do that?"

In reply, Astro pulled his swim trunks back off. "Let's go."

C.C. took a deep breath, reaching for Astro's hand. Astro squeezed back reassuringly, and together they walked out onto the beach, to the catcalls of the Amazons.

CHAPTER 13

ASTRO was pretty much mortified by the time he and C.C. retrieved C.C.'s bathing suit and made it into their tent.

"I can't believe you did that," C.C. said when they were finally alone again.

Astro shrugged. "It seemed like the least I could do since I was part of the reason you got caught in a compromising situation."

"I think you've got that backwards. I'm the one who got you into the situation. It was my idea to go skinny dipping."

Astro smiled. "And it was a lovely idea. I'm just sorry we got interrupted. Now, I think we have some unfinished business."

"You don't have to do this now," C.C. said. "They're undoubtedly still awake and listening. Do you really want to give them more to talk about?"

"Do you really care?" Astro replied, hands sliding over C.C.'s skin. "They're going to assume we finished what we started whether we do or not. Why deny ourselves the pleasure?"

"You have a point," C.C. conceded, relaxing into Astro's touch.

"Of course I do." Astro ended the conversation by the simple expedient of kissing C.C. It only took moments for them to return to the same state they'd been in while in the lake, bodies hard and aching for release. Astro refused to rush even now, preferring to lavish attention on C.C. His boyfriend certainly wasn't complaining if his panting breaths and restless undulation were any indication. Astro kept their lips mated as he stroked C.C.'s skin, muffling the delicious sounds that rose in his throat. Another time Astro promised himself the pleasure of making C.C. beg, but for now he'd settle for the pleasure of C.C.'s eager movements.

Finally, C.C. pulled his mouth free. "Damn it, Astro. Make me come already," he begged, desire turning his voice deep and hoarse.

Astro shook his head, capturing C.C.'s lips again. He could do as C.C. asked, but then he'd be no different than any of C.C.'s past hookups, and Astro didn't want that. He wanted C.C. to understand that he meant it when he said he was interested in more than a summer fling. He wanted C.C. to stay with him, and that meant showing him how good things could be between them. To that end, he lingered over C.C.'s body.

"Can you stay quiet if I use my mouth for other things than kissing you?" Astro whispered against C.C.'s lips.

"I don't know," C.C. replied honestly. "You make me want to scream, it feels so good."

"If you do that, the Amazons will be over here either telling us to shut up or demanding we let them watch, but I really want to get my mouth on your chest."

C.C. groaned from the image alone. "I'll be quiet," he promised, grabbing a corner of the sleeping bag and stuffing it in his mouth to muffle any sounds. For a moment, Astro considered suggesting they leave the beach and hike back up to the main camp, but that would require stopping for at least twenty minutes, and he wasn't sure he had that kind of self-control.

Astro kissed his way down C.C.'s neck, feeling the hint of stubble beneath his lips. That gave way to the smooth skin of his collarbones and then of his chest. Astro took his time, licking across the planes of muscle as he continued to fondle C.C.'s cock languidly, keeping him floating on arousal without pushing for release yet. He finally settled on one pink nipple, toying with it with his tongue and teeth as C.C. writhed beneath him.

"Now, Astro," C.C. pleaded.

With a nod, Astro increased the rhythm of his stroking until C.C. was bucking up frantically into his fist. With a hoarse moan he couldn't completely muffle, C.C. climaxed hard, covering Astro's hand and his towel.

With an eager grin, Astro lifted his fingers to his mouth and licked them clean.

A low growl escaped C.C.'s throat as he rolled Astro onto his back, straddling the taller man, pressing down hard against Astro's hard cock as he captured Astro's mouth with his own. Astro moaned softly, bucking up to increase the pressure. C.C. caught Astro's hips in his hands with a firm shake of his head.

"You had your turn. Now it's mine." Slowly, deliberately, C.C. rutted against Astro's cock. "The way this feels right now? Slow and deliberate and driving you wild? That's how it'll feel the first time I fuck you," C.C. promised. "I'll get deep inside you and then I'll rock so slow and hard until you can't do anything but come and come and come. Come for me, Astro."

Astro gasped and climaxed hard, driven to incoherency by the heated words and decadent friction of C.C.'s belly against his arousal. His body convulsed, stream after stream of fluid shooting over their stomachs. Astro tried to bite back his cry and failed.

"Hey, keep it down!" a voice Astro couldn't identify shouted from outside their tent. Astro buried his face in C.C.'s shoulder as if the speaker could see them.

"They're just jealous," C.C. murmured against Astro's neck, pressing tender kisses to the smooth skin. "You got some action and they didn't."

Astro couldn't argue with that so he snuggled up against C.C. and let sleep take him.

"THERE'S another bad storm rolling in," Scruffy warned at dinner on Wednesday night. "Get your girls settled and then secure your units. Astro, will you and C.C. make sure the staff house and TIC Hollow are secure?"

Astro agreed, joining C.C. and heading out. They checked Yogurt's unit since she and her girls were on an overnight, and then hurried up the road. The storm was nearly as bad as the one the week before but much shorter lived. Astro and C.C. had just started back toward their tent once the rain stopped when Scruffy came racing up the gravel. "Yogurt hasn't checked in since the storm passed," he said urgently. "She took a radio but she isn't answering. We know where she was headed but not where she ended up. Here's a radio. I need you two to go down the Rainbow trail from this end. Rambler and Seuss have already started in from the other trailhead."

C.C. grabbed the radio. "Where were they planning on sleeping?"

"In the meadow on the third ridge," Scruffy said. "Pretty much the most remote spot along the trail."

"We'll make the best time we can," C.C. said, "but there's no fast way to get there."

"I know. Do your best and radio in if you see or hear anything."

They promised to do so and raced for the trailhead, a few hundred yards from the staff house.

The ground was treacherous from the rain, the leaves coating the trail slippery as they left the ridge and started down into the valley. Their feet slid as they jumped over rocks and downed branches, neither of them paying any attention to their surroundings, their focus solely on the ground in front of them and where they would next place their feet. They reached the bottom of the first valley, the trail snaking along the path of a creek bed swollen with run-off from the storm. Astro's heart pounded as they ran along the trail now that the terrain had flattened out, his mind racing with images of the girls or the staff hurt or worse. It hadn't been as bad a storm as the one the week before, but there had been a lot of lightning and wind. If they were out in the open, in the meadow where Scruffy said they intended to go, they'd have been completely exposed to the brunt of the storm. He cursed under his breath as his foot slipped into the water.

"You all right?" C.C. asked, his pace never faltering.

"I'm fine," Astro replied immediately, his voice harsh as his breath sawed in and out from maintaining the grueling pace. "My foot's just wet."

"Let me know if I go too fast," C.C. said as they leapt the creek and crashed their way along the forest floor until they reached the waterfall that marked the ascent to the second ridge. They climbed the steep terrain, grateful for the ropes along that section of the path. They might have made it unaided in dry weather, but with the ground muddy and the leaves slick, they would never have managed. As wet as it was, even with the ropes, they fell several times as they climbed, the rope leaving burns on their palms as they held tight, trying to stop their downward slide. Astro tried to imagine the group of thirty girls, packs on their shoulders, struggling up the incline in the rain. He knew they weren't lying at the bottom of this cliff in mangled heaps, but the Amazons had talked about how many ups and downs were on this trail, and the image of one or more of the girls falling down an ascent like this, with broken limbs, broken backs, or worse, assailed him as he cursed a blue streak trying to reach the ledge halfway up the cliff.

They reached the top of the first climb, skirting the base of the cliff that made up the second ridge. As they rounded the bend before the next climb, they heard laughter and smelled smoke. A little farther along the trail, they found Yogurt and her campers holed up in a shallow cave. Astro sagged against the rock wall in relief.

"Is everyone all right?" C.C. asked breathlessly.

"We're fine," Yogurt assured him, her quiet ease so at odds with Astro's pounding heart that he wanted to shout at them, "but my radio stopped working. I checked it before we left this afternoon, but it isn't working now."

"I'll call in," Astro offered, unhooking the radio from his belt. He got immediate relieved replies from Scruffy and Seuss, along with directions to make their way back to camp at a more comfortable pace.

Astro assured Scruffy they'd be careful but wouldn't linger with night falling.

"Go on back," Yogurt urged. "We saw the storm blowing in and stopped here so we didn't even get wet. We'll finish cooking and get some sleep and be back by lunch tomorrow."

"If you're sure," Astro said.

"Go on," Yogurt assured them. "Get back before dark."

Taking her at her word, they edged back to the rope more carefully than before, slipping and sliding their way back to the valley floor. Almost as soon as they crossed the creek, C.C. backed Astro against a tree, kissing him wildly. Astro returned the embrace, the frantic race to find the missing campers and the surge of relief at finding Yogurt and the girls safe leaving him pumped full of adrenaline demanding release as their lips met and their teeth clashed. Astro tasted blood, his or C.C.'s, he didn't know, but it didn't slow him down at all. He simply angled his head, desperate for more of the illicit contact.

Astro's head thumped against the tree as C.C.'s hands burrowed beneath his clothes, seeking skin and finding it with consummate ease. "Please," Astro begged almost immediately.

"Please what?" C.C. teased, dropping to his knees and tugging at Astro's shorts.

Astro's moan was his only reply as C.C. worked his cock free and licked eagerly at the tip.

"Please what?" C.C. prompted again.

Astro glared down at his grinning boyfriend, grabbing C.C.'s skull and pushing his lips where he wanted them. "Suck me already," he growled.

C.C.'s grin never faded as his lips opened and then closed around the head of Astro's cock. Astro dropped his hands to his side, fighting the urge to simply shove his dick down C.C.'s throat. He didn't doubt C.C. could take it, but even now, hot and frantic and rushed, he didn't want it that way between them, didn't want even a hint of coercion between them. Instead, he clenched his fists and pulsed his hips, asking for more rather than demanding.

C.C. obliged almost immediately, sliding his lips down the shaft until the head bumped the back of his throat. He drew back slowly, his tongue teasing the vein on the underside of Astro's cock, dragging a hoarse moan from his lips. He tried to stifle it and then reminded himself they were alone in the woods. For once, he could make as much noise as he wanted without having to worry about anyone hearing. "More," he begged. "Please, C.C., give me more."

C.C. angled his head, his tongue licking along the full length of Astro's arousal, his head nudging Astro's thighs, urging them to part so he could get between them and draw the heavy sac into his mouth. Pausing for a moment, his hand cradling the balls he'd just been licking, C.C. looked up at Astro. "Did I tell you how much I like big balls?" he asked. "That's one of my biggest turn-ons. Heavy, full, begging to be sucked, bouncing against my belly when I'm fucking. I'm going to suck them dry."

Astro had already decided he had a previously undiscovered kink for dirty talk, at least C.C.'s brand. He'd come several times already from little more than the touch of C.C.'s hand and the sound of his voice whispering provocative images in his ear. "You keep talking like that and I'll come before you get your mouth on me again," he warned.

C.C. chuckled. "You let me worry about that," he purred, licking his way back up to the tip of Astro's erection. "I like watching you come apart as I talk. You like it, don't you? Almost as much as I like your big balls."

"Yes," Astro admitted hoarsely. "When you're the one talking."

"Another time," C.C. said, licking a droplet of fluid from the shiny head of Astro's cock, "I'm going to talk to you until you come. Not today, though. We don't have time for that." Not giving Astro a chance to respond or react, he took Astro's entire shaft into his mouth and down his throat, swallowing around the tip in a move that had Astro thrashing against the tree as his balls drew up tight against his body in prelude to his climax.

"Close," he warned C.C., not sure if his boyfriend really wanted a mouthful of spunk.

C.C.'s answer was to slide a hand between his thighs and fondle his balls until he came hard down C.C.'s throat. Knees giving out, he sank to the ground next to C.C., reaching immediately for the other man's shorts, intending to return the favor.

C.C. caught his hands, pressing them over his cock so Astro could feel his interest but at the same time keeping him from going any further. "It's going to be dark in a matter of minutes," he warned, "and we need to get back. You can take care of me after lights out tonight."

"You always do this to me," Astro groused. "You get me worked up and get me off and then don't let me take care of you."

C.C. shook his head. "If it were half an hour earlier, I'd let you do whatever you wanted to me," he promised, "but we don't want to be out here in the dark, even with flashlights. This is too treacherous a trail for that, and I don't relish the idea of spending the night out in the open."

Still glaring at being denied, however temporarily, Astro let C.C. help him to his feet. They continued back up the trail at almost as fast a pace as they'd come down it, reaching the long, steep climb back to the road while it was still fairly light. The hill slowed them down, though, between the grade of the incline itself and the slippery leaves. "This one needs a rope too," Astro gasped as he lost his footing for the third time, scraping his knee badly as he fell.

"It wouldn't if it weren't wet and we weren't running," C.C. replied, turning back to grab Astro's hand and help him up. He pushed Astro ahead of him, helping steady him up the hill.

Dusk finally gave way to night about the time they burst out of the woods onto the gravel road that bisected the camp. Panting, Astro bent double, his hands on his knees as he tried to catch his breath. C.C. snagged the radio off Astro's belt and let Scruffy know they were back. Scruffy thanked them and told them to have a good night.

Breath slowing slightly, Astro stood upright again. "Does that mean we're off duty for the night?" he asked.

C.C. nodded. "Good," Astro said, closing his hand firmly around C.C.'s bicep and steering him toward the staff house and the showers. The water would provide a shield for any noise C.C. might make while Astro drove him out of his mind.

As they passed through the staff house, Astro flipped the shower sign to "Occupied" so they wouldn't be disturbed and grabbed their towels. He figured they'd need to rinse off at least when he was done with C.C.

C.C. let himself be manhandled out into the shower, standing still while Astro stripped him down and turned the water on full from both showerheads. The water splashed noisily against the concrete slab that made up the floor of the shower as Astro stripped as well, sitting on the wooden bench where they usually set their shower buckets, and pulling C.C. to him. His mouth salivated as he stared at the thick cock in front of him, but he didn't give in and simply go down on it right away. C.C. might be the master of physical seduction, but Astro was determined to seduce his boyfriend on a different level.

To that end, he pulled C.C. down until he could reach the blond's lips, nibbling and kissing them until C.C. was fully hard again. He worked his way down, as he'd done at the lake, licking and kissing bare skin, ratcheting up the tension between them without driving strictly for release. He needed to lavish C.C. with tenderness as much as he needed to make him come.

"I think you have a nipple fetish," C.C. groaned when Astro lingered on the taut nubs. "You don't have to persuade me. I'm a sure thing, Astro."

"It's called foreplay," Astro joked, switching to the other nipple, "and yes, I definitely enjoy it. And if I have my way, you'll develop a taste for it too."

He didn't voice aloud the thought that C.C.'s past boyfriends must have been seriously selfish lovers if they only lingered over him when they were trying to convince him to have sex with them.

Determined not to fall into the same trap—ever—Astro took his time, hands moving randomly over C.C.'s skin as his mouth lingered on

C.C.'s nipples, nipping and licking until they were tender and little gasps were slipping from between C.C.'s lips at every pass. Only then did he let his hand slide lower, to any other typically erogenous zone. His hands settled on the classic curve of C.C.'s ass, wishing his own flat butt was as attractive. He kneaded the muscle firmly as his mouth coasted lower across hard abs to the winged arc of C.C.'s hip. He nipped at the protruding bone, soothing the sting with his tongue. C.C. sighed softly, warming Astro's heart and bringing a smile to his lips. That was the sound he wanted to hear more often, the one that said Astro was touching more than his body. He nuzzled the curls at the base of C.C.'s cock, waiting for another telltale hitch in C.C.'s breathing before turning his attention to the straining shaft.

He took his time even then, lingering over the mushroomed head, his tongue teasing the slit and the frenulum, while his hands continued their massage. C.C. rocked forward, but Astro caught his hips, stilling his movements. Releasing the treat in his mouth, he looked up at C.C., sure his mouth was already swollen from the attention he'd been giving his boyfriend's body. "I promise you'll get what you want. Let me play now and then you can fuck my throat until you come."

C.C. groaned and nodded, bracing his hands on Astro's shoulders. "Just don't make me wait too long."

"Just until you're frantic," Astro assured him.

"Bitch," C.C. complained, but he didn't pull away or try to speed up Astro's explorations as Astro took his time licking every inch of C.C.'s cock. Astro could smell the sweat still from their run through the woods, but the water running over them had washed away most of the salt, leaving only the flavor of C.C.'s skin.

When he'd tasted every inch, he returned to the tip, bobbing his head indolently, taking more of the shaft into his mouth with each pass until his lips were brushing C.C.'s bush every time. Finally releasing his hold on C.C.'s hip, he gave his boyfriend's hard butt a little swat to encourage him to move on his own.

C.C. didn't require any more cue than that, his thighs trembling beneath Astro's hands as he thrust forward into Astro's mouth. Astro relaxed his throat and let the shaft move freely, his tongue teasing the underside as it slid past each time, relishing the flavor that seeped onto his tongue. C.C.'s movements were growing ragged, and Astro decided to see if he could push his boyfriend over the edge. Wetting a finger with the fluid leaking from his own cock, he bumped the tip lightly against C.C.'s puckered entrance.

It had the desired result. Almost immediately, C.C. started climaxing, filling Astro's mouth with his cream. Figuring C.C. wouldn't pull away now, Astro encircled his own cock with his fist, jerking off in time to C.C.'s thrusts. In a matter of moments, he'd come as well, the water washing away the thick semen.

After a moment, they drew apart and washed the remaining mud from their dash through the woods from their skin. As they walked back toward the staff house, towels around their waists, Astro smiled at C.C. "I took your advice and left a change of clothes in my cubby after the storm last week. I'm glad now. I wouldn't have enjoyed putting back on my muddy shorts."

"See, I'm good for something," C.C. joked.

"You're good for lots of things," Astro assured him, "as you've proven tonight. Yogurt and the girls were all fine, but as I was having all these images of them hurt or worse, I was glad you were with me. If anyone would know what to do, it would be you."

They dressed quickly as they talked, heading back down the hill to their tent. Inside, they closed the flaps for the night, securing them against both the weather, which had turned threatening again, and against any inquisitorial glances. That accomplished, they stripped down, aligning their cots and cuddling together, one sleeping bag open wide beneath them, the other spread across them as they kissed languidly before going to sleep.

Chapter 14

THE week passed without further incident, much to Astro's relief. He could definitely do without the drama of storms and missing people and frantic races through the woods. He and C.C. continued to push their cots together at night, sleeping wrapped around each other, but he could sense C.C. holding back as much as he was. They made love with hands and mouths, but neither of them pushed for more. Of course, until they had a day off so he could go into town, Astro didn't have the supplies necessary for them to do anything more. He hadn't asked C.C. if he had any.

When he came back on Sunday morning, having run home for the night to do laundry, he could feel the bottle of lube and packet of condoms burning a hole in his bag. He just *knew* everyone knew that was why he'd gone home. He hid them in the bottom of the trunk the Amazons had gotten for him, not even telling C.C. he'd brought them. Now that they were here, he wasn't sure he was ready to take that step. Things were going so well with C.C. that he was almost afraid to move to the next level for fear of messing up what they had.

All of the girls during the fourth session were young, the oldest only eleven, so Astro expected to have an easy week. As the unit leaders and support staff met to go over their plans for the session to make sure everyone got their activities scheduled appropriately, he realized it wouldn't be an easy week: it would be an empty one.

"We obviously can't take these girls out on the ropes course or on the cliff," he said, "but we could still teach them the basics of rappelling. We could use the slope down to the flag deck as a start and then maybe the retaining wall by the trail house as a bit of a challenge. Otherwise, I'll be bored out of my skull before Friday!"

"I'm sure we could find things to keep you busy," Scruffy said, "but it isn't a bad idea. It would be a new experience for them, but one that would be well within their physical abilities. They run down the slope to the flag deck all the time, and the retaining wall is only about five feet high. Ladies, that's on the table if you want to see about working it in."

Predictably, the Amazons all thought it was a fabulous idea, and so Astro went from having nothing on his schedule to having half his time slots filled. That wasn't as much as the other weeks, when he'd had as many as ten slots filled with either rappelling or the ropes course, but it was definitely better than doing nothing for a week. He could spend the open times taking care of the equipment or joining the girls in non-ropes activities. He refused to let his thoughts wander to other ways of filling his free time. He didn't want to give Scruffy a reason to look at him and C.C. askance.

The week started significantly more slowly for Astro because of the number of first-time campers who needed to learn about the camp and its practices before they were ready for more intense activities. Astro found himself hanging out with whoever was doing a campcraft lesson in safety techniques and general outdoorsman skills. The girls were all delightfully eager, making Astro hopeful the rappelling lessons would go over as well.

"We're going out to the Point tonight," Spirit said at lunch on Tuesday. "Do you want to come stargazing with us?"

"Sure," Astro replied immediately. "I imagine C.C. will tag along, too, if that's okay."

Spirit cocked an eyebrow at him. "As long as you remember to play it cool in front of the campers."

"Of course," Astro replied, wounded she would even think otherwise.

She stepped closer. "They're young girls. We won't stay out too late, and then you and C.C. can have the Point to yourselves," she whispered. "Bring a mat or something to sit on. The rock gets hard after awhile."

Astro blushed as she walked away before he could reply.

"What's up?" C.C. asked, coming to Astro's side.

"Spirit invited us to go stargazing with her campers tonight," Astro said, tipping his head toward the kitchen porch where they could talk undisturbed. "She's apparently decided our tent and the showers aren't romantic enough for us. She suggested I bring a mat so we can be comfortable on the Point after she and the campers leave."

"Is that why you turned beet red?" C.C. teased.

Astro's face grew hotter. "Yeah."

C.C. grinned and kissed Astro quickly. "I love how flustered you get."

Astro didn't have time to answer before C.C., too, had left with a parting comment about teaching basic first aid to Ricki's campers that afternoon. Astro sank onto the chair that was the porch's only furniture, his heart pounding at C.C.'s words.

Love.

Yes, C.C. had used it to talk about something Astro did, not about Astro himself, but it was still a shock, albeit a welcome one, to hear the word cross the other man's lips. Could it mean C.C. was coming to care for him beyond the rather obvious desire they felt? He hadn't dared to hope the attraction would deepen this quickly, not given C.C.'s footloose ways. Maybe it didn't mean anything. Maybe it was just a turn of phrase. Astro sighed. He'd come to camp to get away from this kind of complication.

With another deep sigh, he pushed the thoughts away and went to teach his first rappelling lesson to the younger girls.

He met them at the trail house beneath the dining hall and passed out harnesses and carabiners. They chattered away enthusiastically as he gathered a couple of helmets and a short rope. Given where they'd be rappelling, he didn't think he needed to take all the helmets. The girls could share them with no problem.

Seuss led the way to the picnic tables near the flag deck and got all the girls settled.

"Okay," Astro began, "has anyone ever been rappelling before?"

None of the girls raised their hands. He wasn't surprised, but he figured it didn't hurt to check. "Well, then, this is a rappelling harness," he explained, holding up the article in question. "It goes around your waist and legs and attaches to the rope with a D-ring and carabiner to keep you safe as you go down the cliff. We aren't going to rappel any cliffs today, but we are going to practice the skills. And if everything goes well, we'll try a sharper edge on the wall near the trail house."

The girls bounced with enthusiasm, bringing a smile to Astro's face. He asked for a volunteer, picking the quiet girl in the back when she tentatively raised her hand. "What's your name?"

"Clare," she replied, so softly he could barely hear her.

"You ready to try this, Clare?" he asked encouragingly.

She nodded, her eyes filled with a blend of trepidation and excitement. Astro handed her the harness and picked up his own. "Okay, just do what I do and we'll get you all ready to go."

Clare nodded again and stepped into the leg holes of the harness, pulling it up until it fitted snugly against her hips. "Now tighten the straps," Astro directed, tugging on his own until they were tight. "You want to be able to get a finger in between the harness and your leg so it isn't too tight, but no more than one."

"Okay," Clare said softly, mimicking Astro actions. When that was done, he showed her how to fasten the rest of the harness around her waist.

Catching Seuss's eye, he signaled for her to come over. "What do you want to bet Seuss can hold me up by my harness alone?" Astro asked Clare.

"Really?" Clare asked, forgetting her shyness as her eyes darted back and forth between Seuss and Astro, clearly skeptical given the difference in their heights.

"Really," Astro said.

Seuss got a good grip on Astro's harness, and Astro leaned back, bending his knees and putting all his weight into the harness. The muscles in Seuss's arms strained, but she kept him from falling.

Regaining his footing, Astro looked at all the girls and said, "Now, if Seuss can do that by herself, think how much more secure you'll be when the rope is attached to a tree."

The girls oohed and aahed as Astro affixed a rope to one of the trees. "Ready for the next step, Clare?" he asked when that was done. Her nod this time was much more enthusiastic.

"Good. Here's a D-ring. You're going to clip it through the harness like this," he said, showing her by attaching his own D-ring. "Don't screw it closed yet. We still have to put the figure eight on, but we can't do that until we get it on the rope."

Clare did as he instructed, attaching the hardware.

"All right, last step before you rappel," Astro said, picking up the rope. "Now we attach the rope to the figure eight, and the figure eight to you." He put a crimp in the rope, slid it through the center of the figure eight, and looped it around the other end. Then he offered it to Clare to attach to her D-ring. "Screw the D-ring shut and we're ready to go."

Clare shut the D-ring and waited for his next instruction. He helped her to the edge of the hill. "This is the hard part," he warned her. "You have to lean back against the rope and trust that it will hold your weight. On this little hill, you could probably keep your feet under you, but that won't work on the retaining wall or a real cliff. So what I need you to do is keep your knees straight and lean back like you're going to sit down. You can't fall. The rope won't let you, but it'll feel really, really strange at first."

Clare tried to do as Astro directed, but she moved her feet too soon. Astro grabbed the D-ring and pulled her back up to the top. "Try again," he said. "Don't step with your feet until your butt is at the same height as your ankles."

She was more successful the second time, managing to get mostly in position as she backed down the hill. Astro let it go since the slope on the flag deck, while steep, wasn't the same sharp drop-off of an actual cliff.

Once she reached the bottom, Astro talked her through undoing the D-ring and releasing the figure eight from the rope. She scrambled back up the hill and gave them to him so the next person could rappel. Astro turned to the other girls to see four of them already in their harnesses, ready to go.

"I thought I'd speed up progress," Seuss said with a grin.

In very little time, all twenty-four girls had gotten a turn on the flag deck hill, and Astro decided they were ready to move to the retaining wall. As they walked that direction, C.C. came up the path out of TIC Hollow.

"C.C.!" the girls called. "We went rappelling!"

"Did you?" C.C. asked with a smile for them and another, softer, one for Astro.

"And Seuss held Astro up with just his harness," one of them added.

"Really?" C.C. asked, though Astro knew he was teasing since he'd seen that demonstration before. "I don't think that's possible."

"It is, it is!" the girls insisted.

"Show him, Seuss."

C.C. feigned suspicion. "No, I think I should try to hold him up."

Astro smothered a groan at the thought of C.C.'s hand on the harness at his groin. If the girls weren't around, it would be a different story entirely, but he didn't know how he was supposed to control his reaction. He couldn't very well say any of that, though, so he settled for a quick glare in C.C.'s direction.

C.C. grabbed the harness, his knuckles brushing quite deliberately, Astro was sure, against Astro's shorts. "Lean back," he murmured, eyes raking Astro's body. That sent another flush of arousal through Astro's groin and onto his face if the heat he felt stinging his cheeks was any indication. He sat back the same way he had with Seuss, letting the harness take his weight, wincing a little as the webbing pinched his growing erection. That was certainly a mood killer, but it was probably better that way since he had twenty-four little girls waiting for him to take them rappelling.

After a moment, C.C. rocked him back onto his feet. "Maybe it is possible after all," he said to the girls. "I shouldn't have doubted you."

"Will you come rappelling with us on the concrete-block wall?" Clare asked. "Astro said I could go first again since I did such a good job showing everyone what to do on the flag deck."

"Sure," C.C. agreed, falling into step with Astro as they headed that direction. "You've worked wonders with her," he whispered to Astro as they walked. "This is the first time I've heard her volunteer for anything since she's been here."

"I didn't do anything," Astro demurred. "I just called on her when she raised her hand to volunteer."

"Her instead of the other twenty-three volunteers," C.C. guessed. "Because I can guarantee she wasn't jumping up in front to catch your attention."

She hadn't been and that was why Astro had called on her, but he didn't think it was all that extraordinary. "She did a good job and I want to encourage that," he said simply.

When they reached the retaining wall, Astro scoped out a suitable tree to use for the rope while Seuss and C.C. checked harnesses again. Astro insisted the girls wear helmets this time since they were at greater risk of a fall with a sharp edge instead of a slope. "I'm going to stand at the bottom of the wall instead of behind you this time," he told the girls, "so I can help you get your form right if you need it. You can't fall down because of the rope, but you can fall against the wall if you lose your footing so take your time and pay attention to your form, just like we did out on the flag deck. Ready, Clare?"

The girl nodded timidly as she hooked the rope to the figure eight and the figure eight to her harness. Seuss checked it to make sure the D-ring was locked and then urged her back to the edge of the wall. "Remember," Astro said, "lean back. Don't try to feed the rope through the figure eight. Your weight will do that. You just concentrate on sitting back, legs straight. I'll tell you when you can move your feet."

He kept an eagle eye on the girl as she slowly lowered herself backward, ready to steady her feet if she needed it, but she followed his instructions to the letter, keeping her knees locked as she leaned backward, her feet planted firmly on the edge of the wall.

"Now," Astro said when her legs were parallel to the ground. "Take a step down the wall."

She almost lost her balance, but caught herself before she could fall. Astro, Seuss, and C.C. all applauded immediately. "Well done," Astro said. "That first step is the hardest. Now all you have to do is walk down the wall."

Smile wide, Clare finished the descent.

The other girls clamored to go next, but Astro left Seuss and C.C. to keep them under control a moment longer as he praised Clare's form and gave her a pat on the back that morphed quickly into a hug when she threw her arms around his waist. "Can I go again?" she asked.

"Let's see what time it is when everyone's had their first turn," Astro suggested. "If there's time, we'll do a second round."

That was enough incentive for the girls to cheer each other on and move quickly when their turn came. Astro was careful not to let them rush each other over the edge, but he applauded their efficiency. When they'd all finished, they still had an hour left until dinner. If they'd been out at the cliff, they wouldn't have had time for another time through, but with the dining hall right there, he thought they could make it before dinner.

The last three girls were still waiting their turn when the other campers started arriving to line up for dinner. C.C. urged them to come down and watch since they'd all be doing it later in the week. The new audience added to the girls' nervousness, but Astro took his time with them, encouraging them to focus and do exactly what they'd done before. To his delight, they listened and made it look like a piece of cake for the other campers. The last girl finished her descent just as the dinner bell rang. He shooed Seuss's campers toward the doors so they wouldn't be late, but Clare hung back.

"Can I help put everything away?" she asked. "I don't mind being late to dinner."

"Sure," Astro said after a moment's hesitation. "Grab the harnesses. C.C. will show you where to hang them up while I coil the rope. Then you can put that away too."

"Thank you, Astro," she said, her face alight with delight. "This has been the best summer yet."

CHAPTER 15

ASTRO didn't have a chance to go back to his tent before dinner, nor did he get a chance after dinner because Spirit grabbed him immediately after the meal finished. "We're going to do an activity at the Point before it gets dark. I need help getting it set up."

Astro hesitated, thinking wistfully of the lube and condoms in the tent, but he couldn't figure out an excuse Spirit would buy without seeing right through him. She probably thought he and C.C. had already had sex, but he didn't have to prove her right. Besides, he wasn't sure the rocky Point was the ideal location for first-time sex anyway.

He figured if he came up with enough reasons not to be disappointed, he might actually convince himself.

Following Spirit to the arts and crafts house, he helped her gather sets of dual-colored papers, some black and white, some of other contrasting shades. "What are these for?" he asked curiously.

"We use them to talk to the girls about night vision," Spirit explained. "They think you can't see anything in the dark, but there's actually enough ambient light on the Point from the moon and stars to discern contrast, but not color. We could tell them that, of course, but they get far more out of the experience."

"Sure," Astro agreed. "It's just like everything else we do here. Let them see for themselves."

Spirit nodded. "Far too often, all they get is words rather than experiences. We don't ever want that to be the case here."

"So how does it work?" he asked as they hiked out toward the Point.

"Once the sun sets and it starts to get dark, we'll give them two of the disks and have them try to distinguish the colors. As it gets darker, we'll do it again. Eventually it'll get dark enough that they won't be able to tell the colors but even then they should be able to tell that there are two colors."

"And in the meantime, I'll see what I can teach them," Astro offered.

Spirit grinned. "And hopefully impress C.C. in the process."

"I won't say no to that," Astro agreed, returning Spirit's grin.

"I didn't figure you would. That's why I invited him in the first place."

"We're already together," Astro reminded her. "You don't have to play matchmaker anymore."

Spirit shrugged. "You're together, but is it everything you wanted?"

"Maybe not everything yet," Astro admitted, "but it's more than I was afraid I might have to settle for. It isn't all physical. We do things together simply to be together."

"Good," Spirit said. "There's nothing wrong with it getting physical as long as that's not all it is."

"He stayed and helped today," Astro pointed out. "He could've taken the afternoon off, taken a nap or something. I'd like to think he stayed because he wanted to be with me."

"Definitely," Spirit said. "He's always done anything he's asked to do with a smile, but he hasn't been the type to volunteer for something when he could be catching a nap. Until this summer."

Astro couldn't stop the flush of pleasure at her words. The knowledge that C.C. wanted to be with him enough to change his habits buoyed Astro and brought back his earlier thoughts about how their relationship might be evolving. Astro still wasn't convinced C.C. had meant anything more by his comment about loving Astro than an appreciation of one of his attributes, but it gave him hope of someday hearing the words for real.

They reached the head of the trail out to the Point about the same time Patches, C.C. and the girls did. "What do you have there?" one of the girls asked Spirit.

"A surprise," Spirit said, hiding the bag behind her back. "I'll show you when we get out to the Point."

"What did she want?" C.C. asked, falling in step next to Astro at the back of the line.

"Jealous?" Astro teased lightly.

"Yeah," C.C. grumbled. "She seems to forget you're my boyfriend, not hers."

Astro laughed more loudly than he intended, drawing the girls' attention. "On the contrary," he murmured when the girls had gotten tired of waiting to see what they were talking about. "She's quite happy about me being your boyfriend. She simply wanted to know how things were going."

C.C. scowled at Spirit's back but let the subject drop as they neared the Point. The rock promontory was crowded with twenty-eight people squished together, but they squeezed in tightly and made room so everyone could see the sun setting over the western horizon, the rays reflecting into the lake. It wasn't quite the sun setting into the water in California or the Gulf coast of Florida, but it was still an impressive sight. When nature's fiery show ended, Astro caught the girls' attention and directed it toward the darkening sky.

"Watch carefully," he told them. "If we're lucky, we'll see Mercury in a few minutes, just above the horizon. If we see it, it'll be while it's still twilight. In the Northern Hemisphere, it's never visible in the fully dark sky unless it's during an eclipse."

"Why is that?" one of the girls asked.

Astro smiled and settled in to talk about his favorite pastime. He explained quickly about Mercury's orbit and the Earth's tilt and how that affected possibilities for viewing the planet. The night grew darker without them catching a glimpse of the elusive orb.

"Do you want to see what's in the bag?" Spirit asked, distracting them from their disappointment at not seeing Mercury.

The girls gathered around her as she pulled out a couple of the disks, distributing them to small groups of girls. "Look at them carefully; see if you can tell what colors they are."

The girls peered at the disks in the falling darkness, straining their eyes to make out distinctions. The group with the black and white disk was able to distinguish them still, but everyone else had to settle for saying there were two different colors on the cardboard.

When they'd finished, Astro drew their attention back to the stars appearing overhead, pointing out the Big Dipper, which most of them recognized, and then helping them find the rest of the stars in Ursa Major.

For the next hour, he kept them fascinated with tidbits about the stars, the stories behind the constellations, and the different myths associated with them. Finally, even his storytelling wasn't enough to keep them from yawning, and Spirit gathered them up with a wave of her hand, herding them off the Point and back toward the main camp. She pressed her flashlight into Astro's hand as she passed him. "Since I didn't give you a chance to go get yours," she said in explanation as the last camper started back up the trail. Leaning in closer, she added, "Give us a good ten minutes before you get too loud. Noises carry in the woods and I don't want scared campers."

"My boyfriend," C.C. growled under his breath, grabbing Astro's hand and pulling him close.

Spirit grinned at him and patted his cheek patronizingly. "Make sure you take good care of him," she warned. "He's one of us now."

She had disappeared into the cover of the forest before Astro or C.C. could reply.

"So what qualifies as taking good care of you?" C.C. asked, kissing Astro softly.

Astro hummed against C.C.'s lips, not wanting to end the kiss to reply. The contact of their lips stayed soft, but it was still enough to have Astro's heart pounding in his chest and his breath coming in short little pants when he finally had to come up for air. "Snuggling up with me at night in our tent," he murmured. "Spending the afternoon with me today when you could've been taking a nap. Coming out here tonight and being patient while I helped Spirit with the girls instead of complaining about extra duties."

"That wasn't what I had in mind," C.C. scolded, his hands running down Astro's back to settle on his ass.

"I know," Astro said, mimicking the stance, "but I thought I'd tell you I appreciated them anyway. As for the rest, I've enjoyed everything we've done together."

C.C. rocked against Astro's groin. "Then you won't say no to doing more?"

"Like what?" Astro asked. "This isn't exactly conducive to having sex. And I don't have any supplies with me anyway."

C.C. grinned. "I'm glad to hear you're thinking that far ahead, but I wasn't planning on quite that much just yet. I'll keep it in mind, though."

Astro was grateful for the darkness that hid the heat in his cheeks. "Like what, then?"

C.C. ran a finger over Astro's lower lip, slipping inside and coming away wet. "Trust me; let me surprise you."

Astro didn't hesitate. "Whatever you want."

C.C.'s breath hitched audibly. "Comments like that will get you ravished," he murmured, capturing Astro's mouth before he could reply. Astro didn't think that sounded like much of a threat, though. He suspected being ravished by C.C. would be a mind-blowing experience.

Astro let C.C. move him, taking him slowly to the ground, the rock hard beneath them as they continued to kiss. C.C.'s tongue grew more aggressive with each passing moment until Astro's head was spinning and his breath coming in sharp gasps. Nor were C.C.'s hands still, flying over Astro's body as they did each time they had the liberty to explore at leisure. Before long, they had burrowed beneath Astro's shirt, lingering over his skin. Periodically they would slip back up so C.C. could dampen them between their lips, the night breeze adding to the sensation as C.C. moistened Astro's nipples. Astro squirmed, wanting to feel C.C.'s tongue on the sensitive buds, but C.C. seemed determined not to break their kiss for anything. Even to breathe. Eventually Astro caught the rhythm of breathing through their kiss. He tried to press his own demands, but C.C. would have none of it, catching Astro's wrists with one hand and lifting them above his head. The unexpected feeling of helplessness sent Astro's desire spiraling out of control. He moaned into the kiss, suddenly desperate for more.

That seemed to be the cue C.C. had been waiting for because he released Astro's lips suddenly, pushing Astro's T-shirt up to his armpits, baring his chest completely to the cool night air and the heat of C.C.'s mouth.

A cry tore from Astro's throat as C.C. sucked hard on his nipples, tongue and teeth tantalizing the taut nubs. "God, more, please...." he gasped, arching into the wet suction.

"More what?" C.C. asked, his lips moving against Astro's skin. "More kissing? More sucking on your hungry little nipples? Or do you want something different?"

"Like what?" Astro asked, squirming to get closer to C.C.

C.C. hummed as he licked each nipple in turn. His free hand slid across the bulge in Astro's shorts and deep between his legs. "Like stripping your shorts off and finding out if your ass is as tight as it looks," he husked. "If that's all right with you."

All right? Astro thought it was the best idea he'd heard in a month of Sundays. He planted his feet and lifted his hips to facilitate his disrobing. C.C. took his movement as acceptance because he released Astro's hands immediately, attacking the impeding clothing with both hands until Astro's shorts and briefs were around his knees. He sat up briefly, stripping his T-shirt over his head. "Lift up," he told Astro again, spreading his shirt beneath Astro's bare buttocks to protect them from the rocky ground. "I wouldn't want you walking around bruised tomorrow."

"Nobody but you would see it," Astro reminded him hoarsely.

"Maybe not, but I'd know and I don't want to cause you any pain," C.C. insisted. The words warmed Astro's heart, bringing back once again his earlier thoughts about how invested C.C. had become in their relationship. He didn't know if either of them was ready to use the word love, but he knew he was starting to feel it, and little gestures like C.C.'s care for his backside steadily deepened that emotion.

Then he lost track of such weighty thoughts because C.C.'s mouth had closed over one nipple again as his fingers played across Astro's perineum. "Oh, fuck," Astro groaned when the tip of one finger prodded at his tight entrance. Damn, he wished he'd had a chance to get back to his tent to pick up the lube. Spit wasn't going to provide the lubrication they'd need for C.C. to fuck Astro with his fingers the way Astro wanted. And they hadn't even started yet. Not really.

"I knew it," C.C. whispered against Astro's neck, releasing his nipples in favor of nuzzling the line of Astro's jaw and behind his ear. "I knew you'd be tight. Did your bastard ex never take any time playing with your ass?"

"It's been a couple of months," Astro gasped. "But no, he wasn't much for fingering."

"My gain," C.C. declared, drawing his hand away and lifting it to Astro's lips. "Get it good and wet. I'm going to have to get some of those disposable packets of lube so I can keep one in my pocket for our stolen moments. I have a feeling I'm not going to be able to get enough of touching you."

Astro moaned at the decadent image of C.C. dragging him behind a latrine or into the trail house for a quick fumble, hands sliding swiftly into each other's shorts to probe and tease and provoke. He sucked on the invading digits, circling them with his tongue as he summoned as much saliva as he could into his mouth. He'd need it after the drought he'd been through since he kicked Jarrett out. When C.C. drew his fingers away, Astro lifted his hips in anticipation. The dampened fingers found their way unerringly back to his tight entrance, circling it lightly, smearing his saliva onto the puckered ring. He tried to relax, but that was a lost cause with C.C. whispering dirty nothings in his ear and peppering his skin with light kisses while his fingers played. Finally the tip of one finger pressed with more determination against Astro's asshole. "Yes," Astro pleaded. "Fuck me."

"I will," C.C. said, "but I'm not going to rush this. You're so hot and tight and I'm going to take my time enjoying that on my finger and wishing it were my cock."

"Want that," Astro groaned.

"And you'll have it," C.C. assured him, "but not tonight. No condoms, and we aren't taking chances even if you could take me with just spit."

Astro doubted he'd have been able to do that even if they'd had condoms. Then again, if they'd had condoms, he could've gotten the lube in his trunk as well, but he didn't have the presence of mind to tell C.C. that. Not at this point. Maybe later, when they were back in their tent.

C.C.'s finger worked its way deeper, stealing all thought from Astro's mind as the tip brushed across his prostate. "Oh, fuck," he groaned again. "C.C.!"

C.C. twisted his finger in Astro's passage. "Do you like that?"

Astro felt his inner muscles clench down on the invader, intensifying the sensation.

"Yes," he gasped. "Feels... amazing."

"Good," C.C. said, shifting so he could kiss Astro again, swallowing the moans and gasps that slipped from Astro's mouth. Astro writhed on the T-shirt, trying to get C.C.'s finger even deeper inside him. C.C. teased him, though, never penetrating past the second knuckle, his fingernail skimming Astro's prostate periodically, but not giving it the pressure Astro desperately needed.

"Fucking tease!" Astro protested, tearing his mouth free for a moment.

"It's not teasing if I deliver in the end," C.C. said, suddenly pushing his finger deeper, placing direct pressure on Astro's sweet spot. Astro howled. "Careful," C.C. warned. "The Amazons are going to hear you and come investigate."

That should've been a mood killer, but Astro was too far gone to care about anything but C.C.'s finger in his ass and his race toward his climax. "Give me another finger," he demanded.

"Pushy, pushy," C.C. scolded, withdrawing his hand completely. Astro started to protest, but before he could, the fingers were back on his lips again. "The wind is blowing too hard," C.C. explained. "They've dried off."

"Whose fault is that?" Astro asked before sucking the offered fingers into his mouth again, wetting them as well as he could. C.C. didn't linger this time, sliding two digits into Astro's body. It stung, but not enough for Astro to call off the proceedings. He squirmed restlessly, trying to ease the slight burn. C.C. rolled to his knees suddenly, leaning down and capturing Astro's cock in his mouth. That was more than enough to distract Astro from the mild pain, and by the time he'd assimilated the dual sensation of C.C.'s fingers in his ass and C.C.'s mouth on his cock, the pain had passed, leaving only the soaring pleasure of being filled and sucked at the same time. He undulated beneath C.C.'s mouth and hands, trying to find the angle that brought him the most pleasure. C.C. moved with him as if they'd done this a hundred times or more, until Astro was sure he'd lose his mind. Or at least that C.C. would suck it out through his dick. Even then, his orgasm blindsided him, leaving him thrashing and gasping as he climaxed hard, spurt after spurt after seemingly never-ending spurt going down C.C.'s throat as his fingers kept rubbing against Astro's prostate, prolonging and intensifying his release. When he finally collapsed on the rock, he wasn't sure he'd ever move again. "Damn," he drawled when he could catch his breath, "you pack one hell of a punch, C.C."

C.C. smiled, hand moving on his own cock, peeking out through the zipper of his shorts. Astro wondered when he'd taken it out, but he wasn't about to ask, not when C.C. looked ready to come all over Astro's stomach. He closed his hand around his boyfriend's, the two of them working in concert to jerk C.C. off until he splattered Astro's skin with hot cream. Astro was pretty sure it was the sexiest thing he'd ever felt.

CHAPTER 16

FOURTH session ended and fifth session began without any more progress in the sexual side of their relationship, much to Astro's surprise. Given the way C.C. had talked on the Point, Astro half-expected them to end up fucking at the first possible moment. C.C. had held back, though, not pressuring Astro into more than he was ready for. Over the weekend, C.C. had gone home for a family gathering. Astro couldn't decide if he was relieved or offended not to be invited. They still shut the tent flaps and snuggled together at night, but that was as far as things had gone.

With the new session starting and older girls arriving, including the counselors-in-training who would be there the rest of the summer, Astro was worried C.C. had changed his mind about them.

Until after lights out on Sunday night, when C.C. all but jumped Astro in the shower, sucking and fingering him until his knees gave out. Astro refused to let C.C. get away with simply jerking off this time, using his conditioner as lube to return the favor in kind.

That convinced Astro that C.C. was still interested, but it didn't explain why nothing else had changed. Astro walked around in a constant state of semi-arousal, always wondering when—if—C.C. would suddenly appear and pull him off somewhere private like he'd talked about on the Point. It hadn't happened yet, but Astro lived in hope.

The simmering tension reached a boiling point on Tuesday morning when C.C. joined Astro and Seuss at the ropes course. Thanking his lucky stars he'd worn a loose pair of shorts, Astro forbore to put on a harness himself. If they'd been on the cliff, he wouldn't have had a choice, but the ropes course didn't require he wear one while on the ground, much to his relief. He'd been hard from the moment C.C. showed up.

Seuss went through the course first, giving Astro the opportunity to talk the girls through each element, pointing out pitfalls and strategies to help them be successful. Seuss made it without falling until she reached the hourglass.

Astro encouraged her as she pulled herself back onto the ropes and moved on. The girls all applauded when she finished and came down the zip line. By the time she came down, C.C. and Pluto had gotten harnesses on the first volunteers among the girls. Astro could tell almost immediately that they'd all been through the course before. They moved with far too much confidence to be first-timers.

First time or fifteenth, Astro still talked them through the obstacles, keeping up an encouraging chatter the entire time. They might not need it, but it would help reassure the younger or newer campers who'd never been on a ropes course before.

Much like when they'd taught rappelling to the younger girls the week before, Astro felt his nerves settle after a few minutes of having C.C. around. The awareness of his presence didn't wane, but with C.C. working beside him and not trying deliberately to distract him, the painful arousal faded, replaced by a low hum of contentment.

Despite all their efforts at efficiency, the last camper started the ropes course with only thirty minutes left until lunch, facing a fifteen minute hike to the dining hall.

Astro could hear Seuss getting the other girls out of their harnesses and ready to head back for lunch, but he kept his focus on the girl in the air.

Haley was clearly not one of the girls who'd done the course before, and from the moment she climbed inside the cargo net, Astro could see her nerves. He kept his voice calm and reassuring as he encouraged her to work her way up to the first platform. After a moment, C.C. appeared at his side, calling out his own brand of encouragement, teasing and cajoling. Astro shot him a quick smile, approval and appreciation in one. They made one heck of a team.

"You aren't going to let a bunch of ropes defeat you, are you?" C.C. goaded lightly.

"They're high!" Haley protested.

"So?"

"What if I fall?" Haley asked.

"You saw other people fall," Astro reminded her gently. "If you fall, you'll get to hang in the air just like they did."

"But—"

"But nothing," C.C. interrupted. "I saw you playing Wink with the CITs this morning. You didn't play that hard then to let a little something like height defeat you now."

Astro hadn't seen that morning's game of Wink, but he'd watched enough of the wrestling matches in the game with one person trying desperately to escape her partner to trust that the girl had the tenacity of a bulldog if she'd held back the CITs, all of whom were older and bigger.

The combination of cajoling and goading seemed to work because Haley resolutely fastened her safety line on the balance beam and began edging her way across to the other side. She reached the second platform without mishap, but Astro was keenly aware of the passing time and the fact that Sugar and Spice didn't hold lunch for anyone. Nor were the camp traditions kind to people who were late for a meal. He didn't want to rush her, though. That could result in her falling or losing her nerve and backing out. "Good job," he called up to her. "Ready for the next step?"

Haley looked less than convinced, but she didn't say no, reaching for the next safety line. When she knelt to stretch for the ropes, though, she leaned forward, only to pull back immediately.

"Turn around and face the tree," Astro said immediately. "Instead of going forward, you're going to scoot across backward."

"How?" Haley asked, clearly confused.

"Like this," C.C. replied, sitting on the ground and crab walking backward to demonstrate. "It's the only way I can get across that one either. It's a little hard to get started, but you don't have to look down."

"Okay," Haley called, clinging to the trunk with one hand as she tried to get the other one on the rope. It took her a couple of tries, but finally she started her hesitant way across the cat's crawl. When she made it to the next platform, Astro glanced at his watch. Twenty minutes until lunch and still two obstacles and the zip line to go. They were going to be late.

Haley surprised him with the Burma loops, though. She seemed to grasp almost immediately the skill of moving from one loop to the next, garnering cheers from her fellow campers when she made it across in probably record time.

She stumbled at the hourglass, but recovered quickly and made it to the zip line and down.

"Take the girls and go," Astro told Seuss and Pluto. "C.C. and I will get the gear and meet you at the dining hall. Save us a plate, if you think of it."

"Are you sure?" Seuss asked.

"Go," C.C. echoed. "We'll take care of things here."

In moments, the girls were on their way at the closest thing to a run they could safely allow. Astro bent to pick up the carabiners, harnesses and ropes, hearing C.C. moving around as well, assuming the other man was doing the same. That assumption lasted until Astro felt hands groping his ass. He stood up in surprise, right into C.C.'s embrace.

"We make a pretty potent pair," C.C. murmured in Astro's ear, his breath hot and arousing on Astro's skin.

"We do," Astro agreed as C.C. nudged him forward. He went along willingly, heart racing at the thought of C.C. finally keeping his promise from the week before.

"Did you wear loose shorts on purpose?" C.C. asked, his hands slipping beneath the waistband of Astro's shorts.

"They're comfortable," Astro gasped, arching into the demanding touch. C.C. spun him around, his back bumping hard against a tree.

"They may be," C.C. said, "but that isn't why I like them. They make for easy access." He got his hands inside them again, slipping inside Astro's briefs as well to fondle his rapidly hardening cock.

Astro let the tree take his weight, his hips pushing forward into C.C.'s grip as he felt his head start to spin. "Wh-what are you going to do?"

C.C. grinned. "I'm going to fuck you, deep and hard and slow, until you scream."

Astro didn't think it would take much, not when he was pretty much ready to scream already. He unbuttoned his shorts, pushing them down along with his briefs and stepping out of both so he was naked from waist to ankles. "Please," he begged. "I've been waiting for this."

"Have you?" C.C. asked, pulling lube and condoms from his pocket. He pressed the condom packet into Astro's hand. "You could've asked."

Astro knew that, the same as he knew he'd been waiting for the right moment. He hadn't gotten up this morning knowing it would be today, but now, in the sun-dappled woods, covered in sweat from the building July heat, he knew it was the right moment with a surety he couldn't have explained if he'd tried. C.C. didn't seem interested in asking or waiting for an explanation, though, so Astro simply enjoyed the sensations swamping him as C.C. timed the thrust of his tongue into Astro's mouth with the thrust of his fingers into Astro's ass.

Astro went wild, his hands biting into C.C.'s shoulders as his hips bucked into the probing caress. He bit back a harsh shout as C.C.'s fingernail grazed his prostate, wanting to howl his pleasure, but fearing Seuss and the campers might still be within earshot. Releasing his grip on C.C.'s shoulders, he reached between them, trying to get C.C.'s shorts off as well. The elastic waistband gave easily, stretching around C.C.'s swelling cock as Astro pushed the offending garment out of the way. When his hand closed around C.C.'s erection, the blond broke the kiss, head falling to Astro's shoulder as he grunted. "Careful," C.C. warned. "You do much of that and I'll come before I can get inside you."

"Then get there now," Astro said, starting to turn and offer his ass to C.C., but C.C. stopped him, lifting one of Astro's thighs to his hip. Astro groaned desperately at their groins bumped together provocatively, C.C.'s cock sliding between the cheeks of his ass.

"Where's the condom?" C.C. asked, his voice low and urgent.

Astro realized it wasn't in his hand anymore. "I must have dropped it," he apologized, trying to focus on anything beyond C.C.'s face to find the misplaced packet.

"I've got another one," C.C. muttered, pulling away to reach in his shorts' pocket. "We'll find that one later." He grabbed one end of the packet with his teeth, tearing it open, but Astro took it from him before he could put it on himself, rolling the latex over C.C.'s cock, his fingers lingering over hot, hard skin.

"Fuck, Astro," C.C. groaned. "I'm going to go off like a rocket if you keep that up."

"Not until you get inside me," Astro insisted, releasing the tempting rod and lifting his leg back around C.C.'s hip. Immediately, C.C.'s hands moved to help support him.

A moment later, he felt the tip of C.C.'s cock nudging his entrance. Consciously, he relaxed his muscles and sank into C.C.'s hands, letting his weight precipitate his impaling. C.C.'s shaft was hot even through the condom, thick and hard, stretching Astro perfectly. "Oh, God," he moaned. "C.C.!"

"Am I hurting you?" C.C. asked solicitously, starting to pull back.

"No!" Astro all but shouted. "God, no! It feels so good. Too good. I'm not gonna last."

C.C. nipped at Astro's jaw. "Don't try. I want to feel you fall apart around me."

That wouldn't take more than a few thrusts, Astro mused, his thighs trembling as C.C. started to move again, deep and slow as promised. It wasn't a hard fucking yet, but Astro didn't doubt that would happen soon. He shifted, the rough bark of the silver maple digging into his back, but he couldn't have cared less. C.C. was finally fucking him. Nothing else mattered as the long, deep strokes gained power until C.C. was slamming into him with each thrust, rocking slowly and deep inside before pulling out to slam deep again. Astro's cries grew more and more desperate as he fought the need to come, wanting to draw out the moment for as long as possible. He was sure they'd have sex again, but there was only one first time in any relationship and he didn't want this one to end.

Eyes flashing open as a particularly well-aimed thrust put pressure directly on his prostate, Astro stared blindly at the canopy of leaves above their heads, sunlight playing through the layers of branches, coloring them various shades of green. A bird flitted through his line of vision, the rest of the world going on around them, completely unaware of the powerful congress uniting the two men. Another perfect thrust a moment later shattered the interval of external awareness and brought Astro's attention back to their lovemaking. One more direct hit on his prostate broke his control and he climaxed hard, soaking the hems of their T-shirts with his load. A moment later, C.C. came too, his cock twitching deep inside Astro as he filled the condom.

C.C. collapsed against Astro, his weight pinning Astro to the tree and keeping him from falling to the ground. Astro's leg slipped from around C.C.'s hip, his foot hitting the ground with a dull thud and a rustle of leaves. He hung there, suspended between C.C.'s body and the tree, eyes open but not focused, the whisper of the breeze in the leaves overhead, the dull drone of a nearby bee slowly penetrating his lust-fogged senses. He was in no hurry to move, even as awareness returned, because most of all, he was aware of the thick length softening slowly inside him, and he didn't want anything to speed that inevitable loss of connection.

Finally, C.C. shifted, drawing away and breaking the physical bond between them. To Astro's relief, while nothing could change the physical emptiness, the sense of closeness remained as C.C. tied off the condom quickly, pocketing it until he could find a trashcan. The moment that task was done, C.C. pulled Astro into an embrace again, nuzzling his neck tenderly, and Astro's heart melted as he tipped his head back to encourage the caress.

"Lunch is going to be over," C.C. murmured against Astro's skin.

Astro was pretty sure he didn't care, but he had a group of campers on his afternoon schedule, too, and he needed to pull himself together before he went to meet them. "Don't move yet," he said, ignoring the demands of time passing for a little longer.

C.C.'s lips brushed his softly. "Haven't you realized I wouldn't move any farther away than this if I had a choice?"

Honestly, Astro hadn't realized it, but he was thrilled with the admission. Life didn't work that way, though, and at least their jobs allowed them to spend large portions of their days and all of their nights together. Smiling, he cradled C.C.'s face in his hands, thumb brushing across C.C.'s lower lip. "Let's go be responsible counselors," he said simply, not quite ready to put all the emotions swirling inside him into words. "There'll be time for us later, when the girls are all in bed."

Slowly, making sure to tuck their T-shirts in to hide the evidence, they put themselves to rights again, finished gathering the equipment from the ropes course, and retrieved the condom they'd dropped. As they started back toward the main camp, Astro reached impulsively for C.C.'s hand. Immediately, C.C. twined their fingers together, bringing another smile to Astro's lips. He was pretty sure he'd be smiling for the rest of the day and the rest of the summer if this kept up. Their hands stayed clasped until they drew near the main camp and they could hear the noise from the campers already outside on the flag deck as they finished their cleanup responsibilities.

"I'll go put the gear away if you want to see about snagging a couple of sandwiches for us," C.C. offered. "I'm not all that hungry, but I know I'll be famished by dinner if I don't eat something."

"Sure," Astro said, handing the rest of the equipment to C.C. before heading up the back steps directly into the kitchen.

Spirit was back there, gathering supplies for her camp-out that night. "You're awfully late for lunch," she said with a wicked smile. "Busy morning?"

"We didn't get the last of Seuss's campers through the ropes course until right before lunch started," Astro explained, hoping he wasn't blushing furiously. "C.C. and I offered to clean everything up so she and the girls wouldn't miss lunch."

"Uh huh," Spirit teased. "It doesn't take forty-five minutes to pick up the gear from the ropes course. He fucked you thoroughly, I hope."

"Spirit!" Astro protested.

"You've got stars in your eyes," she told him. "Those aren't there because you talked a scared camper through the course."

"That doesn't mean we had sex," Astro insisted.

"I might believe you—*might*, mind you—if you didn't have bark stains all over the back of your T-shirt," she said, spinning him around and raising the offending garment. "Get C.C. to put something on those scrapes and put on a clean shirt before you go out with your next group or the entire staff will know why you weren't at lunch."

Astro lost the battle not to flush, heat flooding his face at Spirit's blunt assessment of the situation. She didn't sound upset—her voice was too matter-of-fact for that—but he could tell she wasn't as thrilled with the new development as he was. That brought him down a little, but only until C.C. walked into the kitchen.

"Astro needs some first aid," Spirit told C.C. sharply, picking up her box of food. "Take better care of him next time." Before C.C. could reply, she'd left the room.

"What's wrong?" C.C. asked immediately, the concern in his voice overriding any worries Astro had because of Spirit's reaction.

"The tree did a number on my back, apparently," Astro explained.

"Shit," C.C. cursed under his breath. "Come on. Let's get it patched up before you have to meet Yogurt this afternoon."

He led Astro down to the infirmary, insisting he pull off his shirt completely so C.C. could clean the scrapes. Fortunately, he reported, none of them were deep, abrasions more than cuts, but he insisted on cleaning them with peroxide and putting Neosporin on them.

Astro protested the fussing, but C.C. hushed him. "Spirit's right. I should've thought about your back against that tree. The least I can do is take care of you now."

"Stop," Astro interrupted. "Spirit isn't right. If I'd wanted you to stop, if I'd been the least bit bothered, all I'd have had to do was ask you to stop. I enjoyed every minute of it and a few scrapes on my back aren't going to change that."

"Are you sure?" C.C. hesitated.

"Absolutely," Astro averred. "I'll show you how sure tonight as soon as we're alone."

THE tent was dark even with the back flaps open to try to catch a breeze. Astro didn't need to see C.C. beneath him to make love to him, though, his sense of touch more than sufficient to have worked C.C. to a frenzy before mounting him and riding him hard and fast.

The entire afternoon, he'd put up with C.C.'s long face and constant apologies. By the time dinner was over, Astro was fed up and started plotting to prove to C.C. that he wasn't hurt or upset or in any other way importuned by their lunchtime encounter. To his surprise, none of the Amazons waylaid him at dinner, leaving him free for the rest of the evening. C.C. was kept busy with a stream of minor complaints, though, until almost dark. Astro had bided his time, taking a shower and then lying in wait for C.C. to get free. C.C. had been trudging up the road toward the staff house when Astro waylaid him, pulling him into their tent, dropping the front flaps to ensure their privacy, and stripping C.C. in a heartbeat.

C.C. had looked startled, but Astro hadn't given him time to protest, pressing him down onto their bed and straddling him. C.C. had managed to remind Astro that the back flaps were open, but as Astro had pointed out, they looked out into empty woods, and the wildlife didn't care what Astro and C.C. did in their tent. That had been the end of their talking, Astro preferring to express his desire in more physical terms, swarming over C.C.'s body, stroking and kissing every inch of his skin. As dusk faded to dark, Astro took the lube from on top of his trunk and gave C.C. a show, stretching himself until he could take C.C.'s cock. And now he was riding hell bent for release, thighs burning as he posted up and down on the long shaft.

C.C. thrashed beneath him, hips lifting to meet each downward rock of Astro's body, skin slapping audibly in the darkness.

Astro leaned forward, searching for C.C.'s lips, mating their mouths as he reached the pinnacle, losing himself in the rapture of their joining. When he'd recovered enough to move, he laid his head on C.C.'s shoulder, his movements dislodging C.C.'s cock from his passage. "Let me up for a minute," C.C. said. "I need to ditch the condom."

Astro rolled to one side, watching avidly as C.C. switched on his tent light, casting a soft glow over the open space. When C.C. bent to put the condom in their trash bag, Astro lunged forward and nipped the perfect curve of his ass. C.C. yelped in protest, rubbing at the spot.

"I've wanted to do that since the first time I saw you naked," Astro admitted, lying back on the bed, smug satisfaction swelling his chest. "You taste as good as I thought you would."

"I find that hard to believe," C.C. retorted, returning to bed and curling up against Astro. "I must reek."

Astro shook his head. "Not to me. Now, are you done sulking over something I wanted as much as you did this afternoon?"

"Was I really sulking?" C.C. asked.

"Yes," Astro replied firmly, a little curl of arousal sliding through him again at the press of C.C.'s quiescent cock against his hip. He had a feeling he'd be waking his boyfriend up during the night at least once. And if C.C. woke up hard in the morning….

CHAPTER 17

"ASTRO!"

C.C.'s voice was the closest to panicked Astro had ever heard. He sprinted out of the dining hall.

"Get the truck!" C.C. shouted, racing toward the infirmary.

Astro had no idea what had happened, but he changed direction toward the camp's pickup truck, finding the keys in the ignition waiting for him. He pulled it onto the road and toward the infirmary. C.C. came back up the trail, emergency medical kit in hand. He jumped into the passenger side of the truck.

"Get us out to Redwood as fast as you can," C.C. said, panting.

The truck spit gravel as Astro hit the accelerator, tearing down the road as fast as he dared, leaning hard on the horn to warn anyone in their path that they were coming. "What's going on?" he asked, knowing it had to be serious from C.C.'s reaction.

"One of the girls saw a swarm of yellow jackets and was trying to keep the others away from them, not realizing she was standing on their nest," C.C. said. "Rambler said she'd been stung at least thirty times before they managed to get them all off her. She's not listed as having an allergy to stings, but that's a hell of a lot of venom."

Astro shuddered at the thought, fighting to keep the truck on the road and drive a little faster. The moment they reached Redwood, C.C. jumped from the truck, even before Astro had completely stopped, dashing toward the shelter where Rambler and Patches sat with a shivering, retching camper. Astro turned off the truck and ran to join them, not sure what he could do to help, but determined to offer whatever support he could to the other staff.

By the time he reached the shelter, C.C. was already giving the girl an antihistamine. "How long has it been since she was stung?" C.C. asked as he poured baking soda into a small bowl. "Astro, get me some water, would you?"

Astro nodded and went to the spigot, filling a cup with water and bringing it back, not hearing the camper's response.

"Okay, Lisa," C.C. said, turning to the girl. "Here's what we need to do. We need to make sure all the stingers are out and then we're going to cover the bites with a baking soda paste until we can get you to the ER."

"It hurts," Lisa said plaintively, clearly fighting to hold back tears.

"I know it does," C.C. told her, taking a pair of tweezers from his kit and handing them to Rambler. "I gave you something for the pain. It'll just take some time to kick in. And once we get the paste on, that'll help too. You need to hold as still as possible while we work on getting the stingers out, okay?"

She nodded, eyes still teary.

"Do you have a pocket knife?" C.C. asked Astro, pulling his own knife from his pocket. "The dull edge works to scrape out the stingers."

Astro shook his head.

"Here, take mine," Rambler offered. Patches got hers out as well, each of them taking a limb and working over it to remove the stingers.

When they'd finished with all her visible skin, C.C. asked, "Did you get any stings under your clothes?"

Lisa shook her head, her body starting to tremble in reaction to the venom. Astro saw C.C.'s expression tighten as he mixed the water into the baking soda to form a thick paste which he directed everyone to smear over the stings. When it was applied, he wrapped gauze over the mixture to keep it in place. "Okay, Lisa," he said, his voice calm and reassuring. "We're going to get you in the truck and take you to the hospital where they can make sure you're not going to have an allergic reaction given how many times you were stung. It's a good sign that you haven't had one already, but that doesn't mean one won't develop."

She nodded and tried to stand, but she was shaking too badly. C.C. tried to help her, but she cried out in pain at the pressure against her swelling limbs. "Get the truck," C.C. told Astro. "Bring it as close as you can to the shelter. It's going to hurt to carry her no matter what we do, but the less distance we have to carry her, the better."

Astro ran back to the truck, pulling it off the road and up to the shelter. Lisa managed to walk the few steps across the wooden structure with C.C.'s help and get into the truck. C.C. jumped in beside her. "Put the hazard lights on and don't stop until you get us to the ER in Sylva. Lisa's doing great, but I don't want to take any chances with her having an allergic reaction. As soon as we get a cell phone signal, I'll call ahead and let the hospital know we're coming."

Astro nodded and started out of camp, blowing on the horn hard as he went. They hit the main road and he picked up speed, although the switchbacks made it difficult to drive as fast as he wanted to do. When they hit the highway finally, he gunned the engine, pushing the truck as fast as he could. Lisa had stopped whimpering, but he couldn't tell if that was a good sign or if they were really in trouble. He didn't ask C.C., not wanting to add any more fear to the already tense situation.

Astro kept watching the rearview mirror anxiously, afraid they'd hit a speed trap and end up slowed down even more, but they made it into town without incident.

They pulled into the emergency room entrance, and C.C. jumped from the vehicle, shouting for a gurney.

Medical personnel from the ER came running out with a gurney, helping C.C. get Lisa out of the truck and into the hospital. She had gone very pale, her skin clammy from the venom or the pain or simply from shock, Astro didn't know, but she was very obviously affected. They whisked her into the hospital, leaving Astro to move the truck out of the emergency zone.

Forcing himself to stay calm, Astro parked and locked the truck, then pocketed the keys before walking into the ER and looking around for C.C.

"She's in a treatment room for observation," C.C. assured Astro, coming to his side.

Astro let out the breath he'd been holding, relieved to hear Lisa was being taken care of. "So what's the consensus?"

"They gave her a stronger dose of antihistamine to combat any reaction and to help with the itching," C.C. said. "It'll make her sleepy, but as long as she doesn't have any more problems, she should be able to leave in a few hours."

"What a relief!" Astro sighed, slumping into a chair, hands trembling now that the adrenaline rush was wearing off. "I was scared there for awhile."

"So was I," C.C. admitted. "I kept thinking of all the things I couldn't do for her because I didn't have an ambulance's supplies at my disposal. I could've given her that antihistamine myself if I'd had access to it."

"You're not the only one who was scared," Astro admitted. "I didn't know what she needed, but I knew we didn't have it."

"We can't do anything for Lisa for awhile. Why don't we go find the cafeteria? I'm pretty sure we've missed lunch," C.C. proposed.

"I don't think I can eat at the moment; I'm too wound up," Astro said, stomach still churning. "But I wouldn't say no to a cold drink."

THE hospital released Lisa four hours later when the antihistamine did its job, the swelling in her arms and legs went down, and she didn't have any other symptoms. Astro drove them back to camp at a more leisurely, legal pace, arriving just in time for dinner. Lisa's tentmates were thrilled to see her, hovering around her to make sure no one got too close and bumped her accidentally.

They reported to Scruffy, who thanked them profusely for their quick thinking and told them to take the rest of the evening off.

"Seuss and her girls are on a canoeing overnight," Astro said as he and C.C. walked slowly into the kitchen to get dinner. "We could go hang out at the beach and just chill for a few hours. After all the excitement this afternoon, I need the peace and quiet."

"That sounds perfect," C.C. agreed. "We can take a couple of towels, lie there on the sand and watch the stars come out."

"I won't even make you listen to an astronomy lesson this time," Astro said, laughing.

C.C. grinned. "But we had so much fun the last time you gave an astronomy lesson."

Astro flushed, feeling the heat stain his cheeks, but he grinned back. "I wouldn't say no to a repeat of that portion of the evening."

"They say sex is a great cure for adrenaline overload."

"We certainly had that today," Astro said as they wandered back toward their tent to get their beach towels. "You were magnificent today. Utterly amazing. I never would've been able to stay that calm."

C.C. shrugged off the compliment. "I'm glad I came across as in control. My heart was pounding the entire way down the mountain. I was just sure she was going to go into anaphylactic shock and die before I could do something to help her. It's a whole different experience, being in an emergency away from an ambulance and a team and all our gear. I got spoiled this past year, working with the volunteer squad."

Astro draped his towel over his shoulders and reached for C.C., heedless of the open tent flaps and anyone who might be walking by. Their tent was set back off the road anyway. The trees would provide some privacy even if someone did pass by. "She's fine now," Astro reminded him, pressing gentle kisses to his lips, cheeks, jawbone, and ear. "She's got the prescriptions they gave her for the pain and the itching and Rambler will give them to her if she needs them. We'll take a radio if it'll make you feel better, or let Scruffy know where we're going so he can find us if something happens during the night."

"Radio," C.C. decided, leaning into the comforting caresses. "That way we don't have to worry about him coming to look for us and finding us making out."

"Is that what we're going to do?" Astro teased. "I thought we were going to watch the stars come out."

C.C. pinched Astro's butt, startling him enough that he pulled away in protest. "If you start that, we won't get down to the beach," he warned C.C.

C.C. backed off, picking up his towel as well. "Let's go. It's hot in here if we close the flaps, and I really want the privacy to sit and hold you."

They left their tent and headed down the road, taking the fork that led to Sailor Bay instead of the one they'd driven frantically to Redwood that morning. The sun was still well above the horizon when they reached the inlet beach, so they spread their towels out and sat down, enjoying the quiet susurration of the waves. After a few moments, C.C. kicked off his shoes and walked down to the water's edge, letting the gentle lapping roll across his feet.

Astro almost stayed where he was to give C.C. a few moments of privacy, but that wasn't what his boyfriend had indicated he wanted before they came down to the beach and it wasn't what Astro wanted either. Slipping off his own shoes, he joined C.C., waves tickling his ankles. He slipped his hand in C.C.'s, twining their fingers together as they walked in comfortable silence.

"I'm glad you were with me today," C.C. said after a few minutes. "I'd have grabbed whoever was closest, made Rambler drive if I had to, but I'm glad you were the one there."

"Me too," Astro agreed. "Rambler needed to be with her girls to keep them calm and reassured while we were at the hospital, and I know these mountains pretty well. I probably made it down the hill faster than a lot of people could've done."

"I wouldn't have dared to drive the way you did," C.C. said.

Astro squeezed C.C.'s hand. "We've spent enough time thinking about it. Do you want to go swimming?"

"That didn't go so well last time," C.C. reminded him with a laugh.

Astro shrugged. "The Amazons aren't camping here with us tonight. And if you're worried about it, we could leave our underwear on. I really was suggesting swimming, not using the water as an excuse to get naked together this time. It might help you work off some of the nerves from today."

C.C. considered that for a moment before shaking his head. "No, my mind is racing, and I need to get some order in my thoughts. We could've had a life-threatening emergency on our hands today. I'm an EMT. I'm allowed to do more than just administer basic first aid, but that's all I can do because of what we stock here at camp. I need to talk to Scruffy and see about getting some more supplies for this kind of situation. As an EMT, working as the medical staff for the camp, I should be able to have some emergency supplies on hand. I just don't know what I can get without prescriptions."

Astro shook his head, not in disagreement with C.C.'s comment about medical supplies, but with C.C.'s comment about getting his thoughts in order. "Put it aside for tonight," he urged. "You aren't going to solve anything right now. You can worry about it in the morning." Determined to persuade C.C. to do something to relax, he pulled off his T-shirt and shorts and tossed them toward his towel. "I'm going swimming," he told C.C. "Come join me."

C.C. hesitated a moment longer before shucking his own clothes and swimming out to where Astro treaded water lazily. "I love watching you walk away from me with no clothes on," C.C. commented as he reached Astro's side.

"Me?" Astro scoffed. "I've got no ass to speak of. You're the one with the gorgeous rear view."

C.C. shook his head. "Say what you want. I think you're perfect as you are."

"Let's swim," Astro said, uncomfortable with praise for what he considered his weakest physical attribute. He stretched out into a long, lazy crawl, glancing back over his shoulder to make sure C.C. followed him. They swam for about fifteen minutes before Astro felt like C.C had relaxed enough for them to go back to shore. Upon reaching the sand again, they dried off enough to pull their shorts back on, but left their T-shirts off in deference to the heat. The sun was setting, but the night didn't show any signs of getting cooler.

As dusk settled across the lake, Astro scooted over behind C.C., wrapping his arms around his boyfriend and cradling him in a light embrace. "Do you want to stay awhile longer?"

C.C. didn't answer for a long minute, making Astro wonder if he'd even heard the question. "I think so," C.C. said finally. "It's peaceful here, with your arms around me. No pressure, no need to do anything but sit and relax."

"Then we'll stay," Astro said. "Lean back against me and relax." C.C. did as Astro suggested. Astro kissed C.C.'s cheek gently and then settled his chin on the other man's shoulder, looking with him out over the lake. Eventually night fell completely, and Astro looked up at the sky. "Star light, star bright, first star I see tonight," he said softly, "I wish I may, I wish I might get the wish I wish tonight."

He half-expected C.C. to tease him for the children's rhyme, but C.C. didn't say anything, so Astro closed his eyes and wished fervently that he and C.C. would find a way to make their relationship continue beyond the end of camp in less than two weeks. He couldn't figure out where the summer had gone, but they only had one group of campers after this one and then a few days to close down camp for the winter. When that was done, everyone would leave, going their separate ways until next summer. Some of them would come back to carry on camp tradition. Others would go on to bigger and better things, taking a summer's or many summers' worth of memories and leaving behind the impact of their presence on the lives of all the girls who had passed through the gates during their tenure. He knew one thing for certain: he didn't want C.C. to be only a memory.

Chapter 18

THE light from hundreds of luminaries flickered against the growing darkness as the campers assembled in near silence before the closing campfire of the last session of the summer.

Astro didn't know where the time had gone. Yesterday it was June and summer had barely started. Suddenly it was the end of July and they only had four more days until everyone left… until he had to leave C.C. They still hadn't made any plans for after the end of camp, but no one really had as far as he could tell. Everyone preferred to concentrate on the girls still here. They deserved the same experience as the first week campers.

C.C. appeared at Astro's side. "Sit with me tonight?"

Surprised, Astro agreed. They worked together when C.C.'s schedule permitted, but they rarely sat together at meals or campfires, not wanting to give any of the campers a reason to question their relationship. Camp was almost over, though. There wouldn't be another group to worry about finding out.

When everyone had gathered at the top of the hill, they began the long procession down past the pond to the amphitheater where closing campfires always took place. Spirit was already there, strumming her guitar softly as the campfire shed light in the darkening clearing. Astro followed C.C.'s lead, moving to the back row to let the girls sit closer. When everyone was seated and Scruffy started his good-byes, C.C. reached for Astro's hand, scooting closer so their joined fingers were mostly hidden by their legs.

Before Scruffy had even finished speaking, some of the girls had started crying softly. Astro wasn't surprised at the tears, only at how fast they started.

When Scruffy finished, Spirit played the opening bars to the camp song, the young voices of the campers joining with hers as they sang about summer and friendship and the enduring hills that sheltered them all.

Astro's voice caught as he sang the words he'd sung all summer without really thinking about them. He thought about them now, eyes searching the faces of new friends who felt anything but new, seeking reassurance that they weren't leaving immediately. He knew it was only a matter of days, but those days were precious.

The song ended, and unit by unit, the counselors came up to say something special to their girls. Always before, when they finished speaking, they'd ask Spirit for a song and then return to their places. This time, the other Amazons joined Spirit near the fire, sitting next to her or standing behind her, obviously as touched by the emotion of the evening as the campers were. By the time all the units had done their presentations, Astro doubted there was a dry eye anywhere in the amphitheater, his own included. C.C.'s hand never left his as the campfire ended and the girls began to file out in pairs, crossing the friendship bridge with someone special from the week. Astro stood, but C.C. drew him back down to the bench. "Let the girls go now. We'll stay and put out the fire and then we can cross the bridge together with no one else to see us."

It was such a simple tradition, and one most of the counselors had shared with campers rather than with each other over the course of the summer, but Astro noticed now that the Amazons stood together, hugging the girls who approached them about crossing the bridge together but not accepting any invitations. At last, they all went together to the bridge, holding hands tightly as they walked.

When they were alone in the clearing, Astro and C.C. started dousing the campfire, taking their time and letting everyone else get up the hill to the dining hall and main road. The fire finally extinguished, they started slowly toward the bridge. C.C. took Astro's hand as they neared the wooden span.

"I sort of blew this off in previous summers," he admitted, stopping one step short of the bridge. "I'd made friends, of course, but no one I was worried about losing track of. I was already thinking about going back to school in the fall, about which classes I'd be taking and about who I'd be rooming with. It matters this summer. I don't want to lose touch with you when we leave. I want what the friendship bridge promises."

"So do I," Astro assured him. "I didn't come to camp looking for anything, but I'm glad I found it. Let's take a walk."

Hand in hand, they crossed the bridge slowly. Astro stopped in the middle, arms settling around C.C.'s waist. Their lips met in a tender kiss, foreheads resting together even after they ended the kiss. Finally, they parted. "Let's go say good-bye to the girls," C.C. said softly. "We still have a few days left."

Astro ended the embrace and walked at C.C.'s side up the hill to join the rest of the staff. Everyone was milling about at the top of the path where the road widened out at the dining hall. Campers and staff mixed indiscriminately as they hugged and cried and said good-bye. Almost immediately, he and C.C were swept up into the throng, separated by the rush of girls wanting to speak to each of them. He considered resisting, trying to stay at C.C.'s side, but he decided against it. They would have their time later in their tent and over the next few days as they closed the camp for winter. Tonight was their last night with the campers and while the constantly changing faces made forming a lasting connection with them harder than with the staff, he knew the staff made a far deeper impression on the girls, one it was important to honor.

As he hugged girls good-bye and inscribed his address in various memory books, he caught glimpses of the faces of the other counselors. All of them seemed as moved by the moment as the campers were, and he imagined most of them were remembering previous summers and previous campfires, staff who no longer worked at camp, campers who hadn't returned for another summer. His gaze lingered on each of the Amazons in turn, committing their faces and the moment to memory.

C.C. would always take center stage in his reminiscing about the summer, but the other counselors, the Amazons especially, had earned a special place in his heart as well. Spirit must have felt his gaze because she came up to him during a lull between swarms of campers.

"The girls will be here all night," she murmured in his ear. "Take C.C. and slip away when you can. Make the most of the time you have left."

Astro looked around for his boyfriend, finding him surrounded by a group of girls. He skirted the group discreetly, waiting for C.C. to finish saying good-bye to them. They were CITs, he realized, clinging with a little more determination than the younger girls, but C.C. had learned how to establish and enforce his boundaries, and eventually he pulled free, walking casually in Astro's direction. They kept an appropriate distance between them as they moved deeper into the engulfing darkness, away from the circle of illumination cast by the security light outside the dining hall and the myriad flashlights from the more than one hundred campers. A few of the CITs were wandering toward TIC Hollow, the only unit on the same side of the dining hall as the staff house and C.C. and Astro's tent. Even those girls, though, weren't allowed past the end of the flag deck and Astro and C.C. had another quarter of a mile to walk before they reached the path to their tent, so they didn't worry about being observed once they'd passed into the night.

Silence descended as they neared their tent, the sound of the girls, crying or talking as they said their good-byes, fading into nothing until they could hear only the sounds of the night forest: the wind rustling in the leaves, the cicadas whirring their wings, a nightingale singing softly.

"Lie down," Astro said quietly when they stepped into the tent. He closed the flaps, despite the heat of the night, and flipped on the camp light to illuminate the space. "I don't want to rush tonight," he said by way of explanation. "I want to look at you and touch you and taste you."

"As long as I get to return the favor," C.C. said, stripping off his clothes and lying on the cot as Astro had requested. "There aren't enough nights left to waste time hiding."

"After the girls leave tomorrow, we won't have to hide anymore," Astro reminded him, undressing as well and stretching out next to C.C. "I'm pretty sure all the staff know about us, but even if they don't, it won't matter with all the girls gone for the summer."

"Let's not think about that," C.C. said. "There will be time enough for that later. Tonight I just want to think about you."

"Sounds perfect." Astro leaned closer and kissed C.C. gently.

His lips wandered lower, across C.C.'s chest. He lingered over C.C.'s nipples, but his real goal quickly distracted him. Scooting down farther on the cot, he teased the tip of C.C.'s cock with his tongue. C.C. moaned and squirmed beneath him, his hands reaching for Astro. "Turn around so I can suck you too."

Astro angled his lower body back toward C.C., intending to stretch out next to him, but C.C. caught his hips, lifting Astro to straddle him. "This way I get to stare at your gorgeous ass while I suck you."

"My ass?" Astro spluttered. "I'm not the one with a perfect bubble butt. I hardly have an ass."

"That's your bastard ex talking," C.C. said. "I know you don't believe me, so I'm going to prove to you how much I like your ass."

Astro gasped as he felt C.C.'s hands on his hips, guiding him back so C.C. could rub his face against the skin of Astro's butt. He shivered convulsively as C.C. nuzzled and stroked him. Astro tried to concentrate on returning the favor, on making C.C. feel as good as C.C.'s hands and mouth were making him feel, but then C.C.'s wicked tongue found his crack, delving deep, and Astro gave up with a hoarse cry, his head falling forward against C.C.'s thigh.

"You always do this to me," Astro moaned. "You take charge and leave me unable to do anything but whimper and come."

"So?" C.C. said, lips moving against Astro's skin. "I like making you whimper and come."

"I wanted to make love to you tonight," Astro said, voice breaking as C.C. returned to nipping the lower curve of his backside.

"I'm not stopping you," C.C. replied. "Come on, Astro. Blow my mind."

Astro felt the challenge keenly, even as C.C. wrung a deep cry from him with his agile tongue. Astro was tempted to simply let C.C. have his way, but he was acutely aware of how few days he had left to cement their relationship before the end of camp separated them. Their connection had gone far beyond physical for Astro, but he didn't know how C.C. felt other than his rather vague comments tonight on the friendship bridge. Astro intended to use the few remaining days to show C.C. how much he meant to him, in every way he could think of. And that meant keeping his head now and returning the pleasure C.C. was already bestowing.

Pushing up on his elbows, Astro urged C.C. to spread his legs, giving Astro access to the tender places between them. They parted willingly for him, C.C. moaning in delight as Astro tongued his balls.

"You're not the only one with a fetish for big balls," Astro teased, sucking on the soft skin.

C.C. thrashed and lost his grip on Astro's hips for a moment, making Astro grin. Then C.C.'s mouth returned to work in earnest, and Astro realized if he wasn't careful, this would degenerate into a pissing match to see who could make the other come first. Regardless of the outcome, that wasn't the way he wanted the evening to go. He wanted to cherish their time together, to make as many memories as possible and convince C.C. they could make things last well beyond the end of the summer.

Easing up on his attentions, he let C.C. take the lead, licking lightly at his boyfriend's balls and perineum as C.C. drove him wild with his tongue. He'd been rimmed before, but it hadn't felt anything like this. There was something both incredibly powerful and equally vulnerable about giving himself to C.C. this way. With his knees spread wide to straddle C.C.'s chest, every inch of his groin was exposed to C.C.'s gaze and touch in the dim light. At the same time, hovering over C.C. as he was, he retained an element of control he wouldn't have had in a different position. The combination went to his head with all the potency of a strong drink, leaving him trembling as C.C.'s tongue stopped its teasing and pushed past his guardian ring. He rocked back against the invading muscle, unable to hold still as his desire increased. C.C. exploited his restlessness mercilessly, lips and tongue moving unpredictably over Astro's ass.

"Fuck me already," Astro begged hoarsely.

"What do you want?" C.C. asked. "My fingers? Or do you want my tongue? Or maybe you'd rather I push you forward and pound you into the mattress."

"I don't think the springs on the cots will hold up to that," Astro laughed breathlessly. "Give me your tongue. Please!"

C.C. obliged immediately, tongue darting around the exterior ring once more before stabbing deep. Astro moaned as the wet muscle started fucking him in earnest. Not trusting himself not to bite C.C. by accident, he settled for slipping a finger inside his boyfriend as he quivered in need. A hoarse cry tore from his throat as C.C. reached between his legs and wrapped his hand around Astro's cock. Muscles clenching, Astro climaxed hard, spewing over C.C.'s chest. He collapsed forward, panting harshly.

C.C. seemed content to wait for Astro to recover, but Astro was very aware of C.C.'s unsated arousal, currently poking him in the chest. Slowly he pushed himself back up to his elbows and knees. "Turn over," he said, his voice husky, turning around to face C.C. "Let me take care of you now."

"I'm not going to be very comfortable on my belly at the moment," C.C. said.

"Hands and knees then," Astro said. "Just let me at your sweet ass."

C.C. rolled over immediately, lifting onto his knees. Astro fell on him instantly, parting the upturned cheeks and diving between, not spending time now on foreplay. Another time he might have lingered, enjoying the smooth skin, but neither of them was in the mood for slow at the moment, not if the stream of words coming out of C.C.'s mouth was any indication.

"Oh, fuck, Astro, please," C.C. begged. "Your tongue feels so good. Put it in me, please. God, what you do to me!"

Since that corresponded perfectly to what Astro wanted, he didn't hesitate to comply, rolling his tongue and working it as deep inside C.C.'s passage as he could, in and out in imitation of what he hadn't dared ask to do with his cock. C.C. had always been so very much in control of their lovemaking that Astro hadn't imagined he'd want anything else, but feeling the way he pushed back against Astro's tongue, Astro wondered if he should've asked sooner.

That wasn't going to happen this time, not the way C.C. was bucking and begging for release. It was arousing as hell, but Astro's recovery time wasn't quite that good. They still had four nights left together, though. Astro hoped to spend at least one of them with his cock up C.C.'s ass.

For now, he needed to get his boyfriend off. He added a finger, the digit able to penetrate deeper than his tongue could, finding C.C.'s prostate and working it diligently until C.C. cried out his release.

Astro kept right on licking, turning C.C. on his side so he could clean the still twitching shaft. C.C. moved limply at his urging, so obviously replete that Astro smiled and kissed C.C. affectionately. In moments like this, he had no problem imagining a future for them, stretching forward not only through the next year, but the summer after that and years to come. He didn't know how realistic those dreams were, but they swept through him with a vividness that stole his breath. He knew one thing for certain: he'd do whatever it took to make those dreams a reality.

CHAPTER 19

"GOD, I am so dirty I don't think even Seuss could get me dirtier," Patches complained as they finished eating lunch on the second day of closing camp.

"Don't let her hear you say that," Spirit warned. "You know she never backs down from a challenge."

"What challenge?" Seuss asked, joining them at the table.

"Patches doesn't think even you can get her any dirtier," C.C replied helpfully, earning a glare from Patches and a smack from Rambler.

"The idea was not to tell her," Rambler muttered as Seuss's face lit up.

"Wild Walk!" Seuss crowed. She turned to the other Amazons. "One last time, for old time's sake. Please?"

Astro watched in amusement as one by one the Amazons gave in, consenting silently to an afternoon of seeing just how dirty a group of people could get in the woods. Astro had seen campers after a Wild Walk. He could only imagine how much worse it would be with only staff.

"This is your fault, C.C.," Ricki grumbled. "You have to come too."

C.C grinned and turned to Astro. "If I'm going, so are you."

Astro scowled for form, but he hadn't managed to go on a Wild Walk during the summer, having always been busy with his own responsibilities when the girls went. Even more than that, he had no intention of letting C.C out of his sight until he had no other choice. "So when are we doing this?"

"As soon as we tell Scruffy and everyone puts on something they don't mind getting dirty."

Scruffy shook his head indulgently when they told him how they intended to spend their afternoon, but he didn't remind them about everything that remained to be done. Then again, Astro figured he probably didn't need to. No one had forgotten their responsibilities. They all simply wanted to delay the end of camp by a few more hours. In thirty-six hours, they'd already managed to close all the units for the summer, securing the tents and inventorying the equipment in each of the shelters. They'd scrubbed all the showers and latrines, leaving everything ready for any groups who used the camp in the fall. All that remained was to sort and inventory the arts and crafts house, the trail house, and the infirmary, and then close up the dining hall and staff house. They could do that in the two days remaining without any trouble.

He went back to the tent with C.C. to change into his oldest pair of jeans and tennis shoes, not wanting to risk ruining his hiking boots, even though he suspected he'd wish he'd worn them by the time they were finished with the Wild Walk. They met the rest of the staff back at the dining hall and started out almost immediately. To Astro's surprise, Brook and Scruffy joined them as they reached the trailhead for the Waterfall trail. "You didn't think we'd miss Seuss's last Wild Walk, did you?" Brook asked with an amused smile. "Someone has to learn all her tricks for next summer."

The thought sobered them all for a moment, an unwelcome reminder that this would be the last summer all five Amazons would be at camp together. More than likely, only Yogurt would be free in future summers to return to camp if she chose. Spirit, Rambler, Ricki, and Seuss would be going on to bigger things, starting down the career paths of their choice, Camp Laguna a wonderful memory but never again more than a memory.

"Then I'd better make the most of it," Seuss said with determined cheer. "If this is the last one I get to do, I don't want anyone to ever forget it."

The words brought a shout from the other counselors as they followed Seuss down the path to the waterfall from which the trail took its name. Rather than skirting the cascade and pool at its base as they usually did when they hiked the trail, Seuss led them all straight into the rush of water, soaking them all to the skin as they waded through the knee-deep pond to the tiny indentation in the rock behind the waterfall, the undercut covered in deep-red mud. Seuss grabbed a handful of it and began painting the faces of each counselor in turn. "This is clay," she explained as she drew symbols on each person's face. "The Indians used it as dye and to paint their faces before they went into battle."

When everyone's skin was decorated to her satisfaction, she grabbed another handful and slung it in Ricki's direction. By the time the free-for-all that followed ended, everyone was liberally covered in the sticky mud. "Not bad for a start," Seuss said with a grin, ducking back under the waterfall, the flow of water nowhere near enough to wash more than a surface layer of dirt from her skin and clothes.

As they followed her along the trail, Astro smirked at C.C., who had taken a beating with the clay. His blond hair was stained red from the mud. "Looking good, C.C."

C.C. flipped him the bird, making Astro laugh even harder. "Tonight," he whispered, blowing C.C. a kiss.

C.C. laughed in turn as they went on to see what else Seuss had in store for them.

What else turned out to be every mud hole and puddle in the woods surrounding the camp, as far as Astro could tell. Everything had some significance or another, but it all involved getting dirty. Of course, that was the point of the Wild Walk, and everyone took it in good humor.

Even more than the significance of each stop, what struck Astro was how Seuss would leave one trail and strike out through the woods to pick up another trail. Ginger had told him the first day that the Amazons knew every inch of the property, but only now did he realize how absolutely true that was. They knew the trails, but they also knew the lay of the land so well that they could leave the trails and still know where they were.

They crawled through caves, scrambled up hillsides and slid down into ravines Astro hadn't known existed, but Seuss found each one unerringly, and the other Amazons didn't seem surprised by any of the places she led them. The other counselors, even Brook and Scruffy, expressed amazement at the various sites, making it clear to Astro that Seuss really was pulling out all the stops for them, showing them every nook and cranny of the place that had been the center of her life for sixteen years. It saddened him to think of the store of knowledge that would be lost when the Amazons left, but then he looked at Patches and saw the avid way she was studying every possible landmark and thought perhaps it wouldn't all be lost. A new generation would replace the old one and the camp would go on as it always had.

Finally, three hours later, Seuss led them up the final ascent to the main road, out near Redwood instead of near the dining hall where they'd started, but a complete circle nonetheless. Astro didn't think he'd ever been so filthy in his entire life. His shoes squished as he walked. His skin itched from all the mud. He was pretty sure he had leaves in his crack. He couldn't ever remember having laughed as much as he had in the past three hours.

The girls headed straight for the showers, leaving Astro and C.C. to fend for themselves. "Let's go down to the lake," C.C. suggested. "We can rinse most of the mud off and then strip down and get the rest off, enough to put back on our clothes from this morning, anyway. We won't get anywhere near the showers before dinner."

Astro suspected C.C. was right. "Let's go get our towels and a change of clothes," he said. "We'll have more privacy at the lake at this point than we probably would have even in our tent."

Despite the mud—or maybe because they were both so filthy that they couldn't get each other any dirtier—Astro walked close to C.C., so close their shoulders and arms brushed regularly. C.C. glanced at Astro in surprise a couple of times, but he didn't pull away. Astro wasn't quite ready to put his emotions into words, but the end of camp loomed large and he knew he was running out of time. A part of him hoped C.C. would speak first, saving him the anxiety of laying his heart on the line without knowing if C.C. returned his deeper feelings. But if he waited much longer, he'd miss his chance entirely.

When they reached the lake and dropped off their towels and clean clothes, Astro hurried ahead into the water, trying to figure out how to broach the subject of what would happen after camp.

"Hey, what's up with you today?" C.C. asked gently when he joined Astro in the water. "You've been acting strange all day."

This was it; the opening Astro had been waiting for since the last group of campers left. His heart pounding, he took a deep breath and reached for C.C.'s hand. "I'm in love with you," he said in a rush, the words feeling incredibly anticlimactic after all his worrying about how he would reveal his feelings.

C.C. froze for a moment, his eyes going wide. Astro's heart jumped to his throat, every second of silence an eternity. "Really?" C.C. said finally.

"Yes, really," Astro replied, only the waist-deep water keeping his hands from going clammy with nerves. "Is it that hard to believe? You're a great guy and we've had a blast together this summer."

"That's not the same as being in love," C.C. said. "And yes, it's that hard for me to believe. I don't have a very good track record with relationships."

Astro's shoulders slumped. He'd failed after all. All the little things he'd done to try to convince C.C. he felt more than simple attraction and C.C. still didn't get it. "I meant it," he said, "but just forget I said anything." He turned to walk out of the water, all interest in playing together gone.

"Wait," C.C. said, grabbing his arm and pulling him back. "I don't want to forget. You caught me off guard, okay? It doesn't mean I'm not happy. Or that I don't feel the same way. I just didn't figure you'd want to stay with a guy like me."

Astro snorted. "Are you clueless? I've spent the entire summer trying to seduce you into a relationship and you didn't realize?"

"I... I hoped," C.C. admitted, "but I figured it was wishful thinking."

"It's not wishful thinking," Astro insisted. "I love you."

C.C.'s smile rivaled the brightness of the sun. "I love you too."

Astro's pulse raced even more at hearing the long-desired words as he pulled C.C. against him, kissing him fervently. "Don't ever do that to me again," he murmured when they parted. "I was sweating bricks waiting for you to answer me."

"And now that I have?"

"Now I'm dancing for joy," Astro said. "You just can't see it."

C.C. grinned. "Sure I can because I'm doing the same thing."

Astro laughed in pure delight, spinning C.C. in the water with him, his hands sliding over the blond's butt as he pressed even closer. Suddenly, the layers of cloth between them seemed intolerable. Moving to the shallows, he started peeling away articles of clothing, tossing them haphazardly toward shore. It only took a minute for C.C. to catch up with him, seams ripping in their rush to be naked together.

"I've got supplies in the pocket of my shorts," Astro gasped as C.C. grabbed his hips, their cocks rubbing together eagerly.

"Good," C.C. said, backing onto the beach and pulling Astro with him, "because I really want to know what it feels like to have you inside me."

Astro groaned as a fresh burst of lust surged through him. "I didn't know if you'd want that," he admitted. "You're always so very much in control."

"It's a trust thing," C.C. explained as he stopped to pick up their towels. "It's easier to keep a little distance when I top than when I bottom, but I don't want to keep that distance anymore. I want to experience everything with you."

Astro nodded, humbled by the trust implicit in C.C.'s words. He grabbed the supplies from his shorts pocket and followed C.C. up the hill to the grassy bank above the beach. He couldn't stop himself from groping C.C.'s perfect rear as he bent to spread out the towels. C.C. dropped to his knees, leaning forward onto his elbows, butt in the air. Astro was tempted to simply dive between the smooth cheeks and accept the tacit invitation, but he'd spent the entire summer trying to convince C.C. he was different than his random hookups and he wasn't about to do anything now to ruin all his hard work. He fully intended to seduce C.C. properly. "Turn over," he requested. "I want to see your face."

C.C. rolled onto his back, face alight as Astro knelt next to him, running gentle fingers over his cheek and lips.

"You are amazing," Astro murmured. "More than I ever thought I'd find."

"I think we were both hanging out with the wrong guys," C.C. replied as quietly, "because I never thought I'd find someone like you, either."

"I think you're right," Astro said, stretching out beside C.C. and leaning in for a kiss. He lost all interest in talking the moment their lips met, trusting the tenderness and love in his gestures to speak more profoundly than he could in words. C.C. seemed to feel the same because he touched Astro with a reverence previously absent as they reclined side by side, hands brushing as they kissed. Neither of them was inclined to rush, the distance from the staff house and dining hall ensuring their privacy. They lingered over the preliminaries, caressing and kissing, whispering praise and love in each other's ears as they touched and licked and nuzzled. Astro watched C.C. struggle against the need to take charge, soothing him with tender kisses and promises of the pleasures to come. Pushing up onto his knees again, he nibbled down C.C.'s torso, across his tight belly until he reached the curve of C.C.'s hip and the eager cock that leaked steadily into its nest of curls.

He took the tip in his mouth, sucking lightly as he slid his fingers between C.C.'s parted thighs to cradle the pendant sac, massaging it lightly. C.C. bucked up, obviously wanting more, but Astro didn't immediately comply, keeping his lips closed around the head of C.C.'s cock rather than working down the shaft. He did sweep his tongue across the weeping slit, enjoying the salty flavor as C.C. moaned hoarsely above him. Shifting so he could balance without either hand, Astro let his free hand work between C.C.'s cheeks, trailing teasingly up and down the dark cleft. C.C. cried out each time Astro's fingers brushed across his entrance. Smiling around the cock in his mouth, Astro shortened his strokes until his fingers simply settled on the puckered flesh and C.C. was begging constantly, a mostly incoherent string of moans, cries, and Astro's name.

Releasing C.C.'s balls on the theory that his boyfriend would rather have Astro move that hand than the one fingering him, Astro felt around blindly for the packet of lube he'd dropped next to the towel. Finding it, he slicked his fingers and penetrated the flesh he'd been teasing, feeling C.C.'s heat close around him. He'd only managed to do this a couple of times before, C.C. usually taking control the moment Astro started playing with his ass, but this time C.C. didn't pull away—wouldn't pull away—so Astro took his time, stretching the guardian ring carefully, sliding two fingers in and out languidly, deliberately avoiding C.C.'s prostate. He could tell his boyfriend was on edge and he wasn't ready for this to be over yet. He could probably get C.C. hard again, but that might be a stretch for his own patience. Better to keep C.C. just this side of release until Astro was ready to join him.

Finally, his own cock throbbing, Astro rolled on a condom, releasing C.C.'s cock with an audible pop. "About fucking time," C.C. grumbled, lifting his hips to meet Astro's.

"Always in a rush," Astro teased, grinding against C.C.'s entrance without penetrating. "You need to learn the joys of anticipation."

"Fuck anticipation," C.C. growled, grabbing Astro's cock and lining it up with his entrance. "Fuck me instead."

Astro pushed forward slowly, not sure how long it had been since C.C. last bottomed. The tight heat engulfed him immediately, even through the barrier of the condom, making him wish he could feel it on bare skin. That was premature, but maybe someday, when they'd been together for more than two months—he couldn't believe that was all it had been—they'd be ready to get tested and do without the latex sheath.

For now, though, he'd treasure the simple fact that C.C. let him inside at all.

"You feel so good inside me," C.C. whispered, pulling Astro down for a kiss, "so hot and hard and eager for me. I want to feel you moving inside me, splitting me in two."

The words shattered Astro's control and his hips snapped forward, burying himself so deep inside C.C.'s body that their skin slapped together audibly.

"Yes," C.C. groaned, "like that. So deep and hard I'll feel it for a week."

Astro choked back a sob as he began to move, trying to retain some modicum of control. It would be so easy to give in and fuck C.C. until he came, but he wanted more than that. He wanted to make love with his boyfriend, knowing they were in love and that their joining meant more than mere release.

C.C. didn't stop the barrage of encouraging words, but Astro found it far easier to maintain the languorous pace that he expected. C.C.'s pleas fired his blood, but still he continued the slow rhythm of thrust and withdrawal intended to prolong their lovemaking as long as possible.

When he felt his control begin to waver, he worked a hand between their bellies, circling C.C.'s cock and stroking it in time with his pulsing hips. It only took a moment for C.C. to start climaxing around him, massaging his length with every contraction of strong muscles, milking his own release from him in long, stuttering waves.

He collapsed on top of C.C., senses reeling as he tried to assimilate the mind-blowing orgasm and the incredible feeling of connection that accompanied it. Lifting his head, he nuzzled C.C.'s slack jaw. "Love you."

C.C. hummed softly. "Love you too."

Chapter 20

EVERYTHING was done.

Sugar and Spice had left cereal and milk for breakfast, but after that, they were done, released, free. Except it didn't feel like freedom. It felt like a death knell for the friendships of the summer.

They debated over dinner where to spend their final evening together, whether they should go down to the amphitheater where the closing campfires always took place or whether they should gather in one of the units where they'd have a more intimate setting. "Why not go back out to the Point?" C.C suggested. "I know it's not traditional but it's where we began the summer. Why not end it there as well?"

No one had any objections, so as soon as they finished cleaning up from dinner, Spirit grabbed her guitar and they walked slowly toward the Point. With the girls gone and with them the need for secrecy, Astro took C.C.'s hand as they walked. They gathered in near silence on the Point as Seuss and Ricki built the fire, and Astro felt the same weightiness of place come over him that he'd always felt in the amphitheater during the closing campfires. For the next few hours, they occupied sacred space, even if no one outside the people silently circling the fire would recognize it that way.

When the flames leapt skyward, Spirit began strumming her guitar, singing the favorite song of each counselor in turn, pausing between songs for Scruffy to give each counselor an award. Most of them were humorous, intended to evoke the person's quirks and bring a smile to everyone's face as they remembered the incidents that contributed to the award. A few of them were poignant, particularly for the staff who wouldn't be returning the following summer. Astro grinned down at the plaque in his hand inscribed with the words Tarzan Award. He never did make it all the way to the end of the zip line, but he'd tried his best every time he completed the ropes course. He grinned even more when he thought about C.C.'s Nature Boy award for his preference for swimming *au naturel*. He wondered if the Amazons had told Brook and Scruffy about their revenge. He was pretty sure no one else knew about the other two times he and C.C. had gone skinny-dipping.

When Scruffy had given awards to all the support staff and junior counselors and only the Amazons remained, Astro reached for C.C.'s hand again, sure the next few minutes would be heart-wrenching. Spirit began with Rambler, singing her favorite song quietly. Astro watched tears form in Rambler's eyes as Spirit's voice gave tribute to the friend of her childhood and adolescence. When she was done, Scruffy gave Rambler a plaque that named her queen of the Rainbow Trail.

Spirit turned to Yogurt next, offering the same tribute through music, followed by a plaque from Scruffy naming her the official milkmaid of the camp since she was the only one who could change the milk bags in the machine without spilling. That brought as much laughter as it did tears.

Ricki received the Camp Mother award for her extraordinary patience with the younger campers. Seuss got the Wild Walk Wonder Woman award, eliciting another round of laughter.

"You can't play your own song," Patches said when Scruffy had finished with the other Amazons. "I don't play as well as you do, but I play well enough for this."

Spirit nodded, eyes sparkling with unshed tears as she handed her guitar to Patches. The girl's voice trembled as she began to sing Joni Mitchell's *Circle Game*. When she reached the first chorus, Astro's breath caught at how appropriate the words were. As Patches sang about the seasons going around and the carousel of time, he saw it playing out before his very eyes. One group of counselors was leaving, to be replaced but never forgotten by a younger group.

"I tried to come up with a better award than last year," Scruffy said when Patches had finished singing, "but I couldn't come up with anything more appropriate. So here's your second Have Song, Will Sing award. This old place won't be the same without you five next summer."

Spirit reached for her guitar, and Patches handed it back, letting her retreat behind the safety net it represented.

"We have one other thing for our Amazons," Patches said softly, her voice trembling. Astro held his breath, hoping his friends would see their gesture as the tribute it was intended to be. "This morning, Astro, C.C., and I retraced the Wild Walk from this week and marked the trail. We don't have the official trailhead markers yet, but Scruffy's ordered them. The new trail will officially be called the Amazon trail."

The tears flowed openly down the faces of the five Amazons as Patches gave each of them a tight hug. "You were counselors-in-training my first summer as a camper," she went on, her voice breaking. "And you were larger than life, everything I could ever aspire to be. My mother warned me the next summer not to be disappointed if you weren't back, but I couldn't believe that would happen. I couldn't imagine this place without you. I didn't have to because you were there, that summer and every summer since. And you're still larger than life to me. I don't know what I'll do next summer without you."

Spirit smiled through the tears streaming down her face. "You'll be us," she assured Patches. "You may not feel like it—we never did—but you'll be that larger-than-life figure to another generation of girls who won't know us, but will know what it means to come to Camp Laguna and find the friendship and sisterhood we've all come to associate with these hills. And in a few years, when your reign here is done, you'll pass the title to another generation of counselors, just as was done for us and as we're doing for you. That's the beauty of this place. It endures."

After that, there wasn't anything else to say. Not even trying to staunch her tears, Spirit began the camp song, the tribute to the place that had sheltered them all for the summer and given birth to so many friendships. They all sang through the first verse, Seuss and Ricki weaving the harmony in with the melody carried by the other voices. As they began the chorus, Astro felt C.C. squeeze his hand and turned to meet his boyfriend's eyes. The expression in them, even shadowed by the falling darkness and the firelight, stole Astro's breath.

"I add my breath to your breath that we may be as one person. May our days on earth be long. May we finish our road together," C.C. sang, not for the staff as a whole, but for Astro. The others continued on with the song, but C.C. stopped, his eyes begging Astro to agree, to reiterate the promise they'd made on the friendship bridge.

To give their fledgling love a chance to flourish away from the insular world of camp.

"Yes," Astro mouthed silently, hoping C.C. could read his agreement in the movement of his lips and the expression on his face. Time seemed to stretch as a smile spread across C.C.'s face and he leaned in to kiss Astro quickly. When they separated and Astro's attention returned partially to the rest of the staff and the music still surrounding them, he realized it couldn't have been more than a few seconds given where they were in the song. He scooted a little closer to C.C., his arm slipping around the other man's waist. C.C. leaned into him, resting his head on Astro's shoulder, widening Astro's smile even more. Yes, camp was ending tomorrow, but he finally knew his relationship with C.C. wouldn't end with it.

The song ended and silence fell again, but no one moved to fill it or to begin the long walk back to the staff house.

Eventually, Seuss broke the silence. "You know, C.C., since we won't be back next summer, you really should tell us what your nickname stands for."

C.C. shifted uncomfortably in Astro's arms, straightening slightly. Astro loosened his embrace, but didn't let go. "It doesn't apply anymore," C.C. insisted, his voice betraying his unease. "It was a joke at another camp that never really applied here. Now it won't ever apply again."

"Let it go, Seuss," Ricki said quietly. "It doesn't matter anyway. Whatever it stood for before, he's simply C.C. now."

Seuss looked like she wanted to insist, but after a moment, she nodded and dropped the matter. Her words, though, had broken the spell that held them all in the moment. A few at a time, the counselors began rising and returning down the path toward the road and the staff house. C.C. made no move to rise, so Astro stayed where he was as well, until only he and C.C., the Amazons, and a few of the younger counselors remained. Rambler looked skyward at the wash of stars that had come out while they sang and laughed and cried. "I'm glad you were here this summer," she said to Astro. "You and C.C. brought knowledge and experience the rest of us didn't have. I hope you'll come back at least one more summer and share it with the girls again."

Astro didn't have an answer, not knowing where he'd be next summer or what his path would hold, but he knew a part of him was inextricably tied to Camp Laguna. The desire to return would remain even if it was never fulfilled.

The fire burned low, but no one added any wood to it, content to let it die down naturally, much the way the summer had done. When nothing but coals remained, C.C. leaned back against Astro and whispered, "Let's leave them alone. They deserve to say their good-byes in private."

Astro nodded and rose, tapping Patches on the shoulder to encourage her to come with them. Her eyes darted back and forth between the two men and the Amazons, but finally she stood as well, leaving the five friends to make their final farewells.

Patches continued on up the road to the staff house when Astro and C.C. stopped at the path down to their tent. "See you in the morning?" she asked softly.

"We won't leave without saying good-bye to everyone," Astro promised. They walked down the narrow path, no longer needing to look at the ground to avoid the roots that could trip them up. Astro knew he would probably never approach the Amazons' knowledge of the camp, but he didn't need a flashlight to navigate his own little corner of it anymore.

They closed the front flaps of the tent, though Astro doubted anyone would disturb them tonight of all nights, and started undressing slowly in the dim light from C.C.'s lantern. "Cabin Crawler," C.C. said quietly.

"What?" Astro asked, not following C.C.'s tangent.

"That's what C.C. stands for," C.C. said. "At a previous camp, I had a bit of a reputation, mostly unfounded, honestly, but the nickname stuck and then got abbreviated to C.C. so it wouldn't scandalize the younger kids."

Astro sat down on the pushed-together cots. "Thank you for telling me," he said honestly. "You didn't have to any more than you had to tell the Amazons."

C.C. shrugged. "You deserve to know. I told you I didn't have much of a track record with relationships, but I want to make ours work, Astro. I hope you can believe that."

"I do," Astro assured him, realizing C.C.'s revelation hadn't changed anything about his feelings. It wasn't like he hadn't known C.C. slept around a lot before they met. Even after they met, before they got together. "We leave in the morning," he added unnecessarily.

"I know," C.C. said. "I'm not ready."

"Me, either," Astro admitted. "Are you going all the way home to Wilmington or are you staying in the area until classes start?"

"I have to go back to Wilmington eventually to see my parents for a few days," C.C. answered, "but I didn't tell them when I was coming. Maybe... maybe you could come with me?"

The rush of words brought a smile to Astro's face. "I'd love to. I have some pre-orientation stuff to take care of next week, but maybe next weekend?"

C.C. smiled beatifically. "I'll call my mom tomorrow when I get back to my place on campus. My roommate sublet it over the summer, but the other guy left last weekend."

Astro hid his disappointment. He'd been hoping C.C. wouldn't have a place to stay so he could invite him to come stay at Astro's place until classes started back up. "Great. We'll be able to see each other fairly easily."

"Saturday night, at the same bar we went to with the Amazons for Yogurt's birthday," C.C. said impulsively. "Meet me there at eight?"

"You're on," Astro said with a grin. He tugged on C.C.'s hand, bringing his boyfriend onto the bed beside him. He shifted around until C.C.'s head rested on his chest, their bodies pressed together all the way down to their toes.

They lay like that for a long time, the sense of rightness so strong that Astro finally had to speak.

"I'll miss sleeping in your arms," he whispered. "I know we have to leave, but I don't know if I'll be able to give it up for long."

A quiet snore was C.C.'s only reply. Astro considered waking him for a moment, then let it go. They had a date on Saturday. He'd gotten this far by letting C.C. come to his own realizations rather than pressing the issue. It wouldn't hurt to leave some things undecided for a little longer.

THE drive down the mountain was nearly as harrowing as the drive up nine weeks earlier, not because of the road itself or because of any fears about what Astro would find at the other end, but for the very reason that he knew what was at the other end, and at the moment, that didn't include C.C. Yes, they had their date planned for Saturday night, in some ways far more than Astro had dared to hope for at the beginning of their relationship, but it wouldn't be the same. It couldn't be the same. He knew that and accepted it, but a part of him couldn't help but mourn the easy closeness they'd developed.

The temperature rose as the elevation fell, until he rolled up the windows and turned on the air conditioning in self-defense. He clung to the memory of C.C. holding him close after they finished closing their tent, lashing everything down. They had whispered words of love and promises to see each other on Saturday, and to call or text between now and then. Astro had all the ways he could possibly need to get in touch with his boyfriend except the reach of his hand, the only way he'd needed all summer long. He simply had to accept that camp was a time and place outside of time, where all the normal rules didn't apply. Saturday was only a few days away. He could stand it until then.

With a muffled snort, he reached for his cell phone and dialed C.C.'s number. It flipped straight to voice mail, but just hearing C.C.'s voice helped. "This is Sam. Leave a message."

"I miss you already. Love you."

EPILOGUE

ASTRO stood right inside the door of the bar where he was supposed to meet C.C., watching his boyfriend waiting for him. He was early, having missed C.C. to the point of constant distraction, but C.C. had gotten there even earlier, long enough to have attracted some attention, apparently. Astro watched in amusement as a guy came up to C.C., obviously trying to strike up a conversation. C.C.'s expression remained polite, but it was quickly clear he was giving the guy the brush-off. A few minutes later, another one took the first guy's place. C.C.'s reaction was equally dismissive.

Smiling to himself, Astro decided it was time to stake his claim. Striding across the dance floor with the confidence of one sure of his welcome, he slipped his arms around C.C. from behind, before the other man had completely given up. C.C. leaned back into his embrace immediately, turning his head to meet Astro's lips in an ardent kiss. "Hi, Sam," Astro murmured when they separated, laughing at the unfamiliar name. "That's never going to work. You'll always be C.C. to me."

"That's okay with me," C.C. replied with a matching grin. "I wasn't planning on calling you Roger. Astro suits you much better."

That little bit of awkwardness out of the way, Astro signaled the bartender and ordered a drink for himself and another one for C.C. "How've you been?" he asked when the drinks were delivered.

"Not bad," C.C. said. "I got all the classes I wanted for the fall, including one at UNC-A, so I'll be on campus up there twice a week. What about you?"

"All registered for classes," Astro said. "Do you find it hard to remember to flush the toilet?"

C.C. laughed. "Yes! I go through that at the end of every summer. Just like I have a hard time getting used to the sound of the air conditioner and the fridge and all the background noises of modern life. And I talked to my professor. He wants me as his teaching assistant again this fall, so that's good. I won't have to find another work study for my financial aid."

"That's good," Astro said. "I haven't heard anything about mine yet. Hopefully something will turn up soon, though. My paycheck from camp will only stretch so far."

"Isn't that the truth?" The conversation tapered off after that, each of them sipping their drink, trying to figure out what to say next.

"I missed you," C.C. said after a moment. "I've gotten used to having you around all the time."

"I missed you too," Astro assured him. "I know this is maybe premature, but one of my roommates called this morning to say he'd found another place to live, closer to campus, rather than out in Marshall. It's only a twenty-minute drive from town. I was hoping you might be interested in taking his place. It's a three-bedroom, so you could have your own room if you wanted, but I was kind of hoping, well...."

"I'd love to move in with you," C.C. finished for him. "I've been miserable without you."

"That will probably get easier when we get back into our old lives," Astro felt compelled to point out.

C.C. shook his head. "I don't want it to get easier and I don't want to go back to the way things were before I met you. I want us to be together."

Astro grinned. "Do you really want to stay here or would you rather go back to my place?"

C.C.'s smile rivaled the strobe light overhead. "Take me home."

Ariel Tachna

ARIEL TACHNA lives in southwestern Ohio with her husband, her daughter and son, and their cat. A native of the region, she has nonetheless lived all over the world, having fallen in love with both France, where she found her career and her husband, and India, where she dreams of retiring some day. She started writing when she was twelve and hasn't looked back since. A connoisseur of wine and horses, she's as comfortable on a farm as she is in the big cities of the world.

Visit Ariel's web site at http://www.arieltachna.com/ and her blog at http://arieltachna.livejournal.com/.

Other titles by ARIEL TACHNA

http://www.dreamspinnerpress.com

 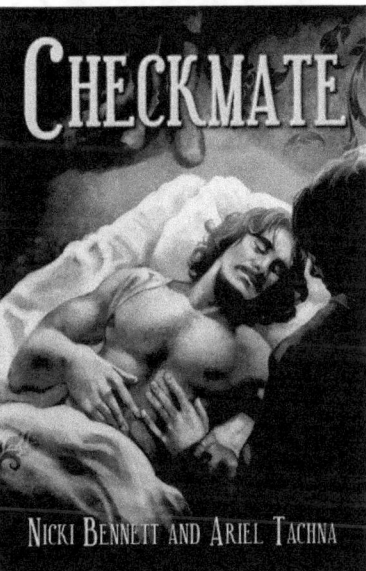

http://www.dreamspinnerpress.com

www.ingramcontent.com/pod-product-compliance
Lightning Source LLC
Chambersburg PA
CBHW070010260626
47159CB00005B/1740